THE JOURNAL OF
NICHOLAS THE AMERICAN

by the same author

FACES

The Journal of
Nicholas the American

Leigh Kennedy

Irwin Publishing
Toronto Canada

Copyright © 1986 Leigh Kennedy

Canadian Cataloguing in Publication Data

Kennedy, Leigh, 1951–
The Journal of Nicholas the American

ISBN 0–7725–1622–7

I. Title.

PS3561.E565J68   1986   813'.54   C86–094113–2

1 2 3 4 5 6 7 8   93 92 91 90 89 88 87 86

Published by Irwin Publishing Inc.

Printed in Great Britain

17 February

Papa visited me last night. I am thinking that I may have to hide now.

Once again, someone has discovered us – he's looking for the family, looking for the *pozhar-golava*. When I was small, a man came looking for old scandal. He didn't know that dealing with Fyodor Nicholaevich was like trying to fool yourself. Grandfather (my Papa told me once) had him figured out in a moment; he knew he could lie to him, and he did. No, the Dals were city people, from Petrograd – oh, no, we must call it Leningrad now, eh? The man was a refugee from the Hungarian Uprising in 1957, still new to America. Grandfather snowed him with political talk, but if he had been from the Soviet Union, all the lies would have been transparent.

The search for *pozhar-golava* was forgotten – obviously our family had nothing to do with strange powers and bloody nights.

When I got home from class yesterday, I knew that Papa was in my apartment, I felt him there as I wheeled my bicycle into the garage. I picked up the vodka bottle that I had tossed down onto the grass from the top of my steps last week when I'd been drinking. My landlady never seemed to notice such things, but I felt guilty.

As I got out my key – I don't know why I always pretend ignorance about my father's presence – he was already saying hello in his way.

'Papa,' I said, and set my texts on the bookshelves inside the door, then carried my package to the kitchen.

'How are you, Kolya?'

'Fine, fine.' I opened the cupboard in my tiny kitchen and took down two glasses.

My father stood in the doorway. 'Can't we talk first?'

I could feel him probing into me. I've never been resistant to him, and didn't want him worming through me. He was lonely. He was afraid of me. All as usual. I couldn't bear even half an hour of this.

'Please. Drink with me,' I said. I balled up the paper bag and threw it against the wall. He knew I was angry. I've told him so many times to warn me about his visits, but, no, he will never learn American manners. I poured us each a glass of vodka and handed him one.

He sighed and took a long swallow. I saluted him. He smiled and returned the salute. We drank and I refilled the plastic glasses. It was warm, I could feel it begin to scrub me clean.

'Have you seen Grandmama lately?' I asked.

'How are your studies?' From his evasion I understood that he hadn't been home for a long time.

'Some day I'll finish. Let's go sit.'

My father and I sat on my bed – or, rather, the mattresses on the floor. I noticed a parcel sitting on the pillow, but didn't ask about it. He looked tired. Sometimes when I look at him, I think I see the flour of his bakery in the creases around his eyes, in the temples of his hair, but it is only age. My father looks old and tired now.

We drank for a moment, and relaxed.

'Have you been drinking a lot?' he asked.

'No. This is the first time since last week. I have to study, so I stop during the week. It's quiet here, anyway. The landlady,' I pointed downstairs, 'is a mouse. She doesn't disturb me. I feel good now, things are working out. Maybe next spring I'll start graduate school.'

'Good,' Papa said vaguely.

'And you? Any new lady friends now?'

'Had one. I think I told you about her. She was too – *wild*,' he said, using the English word. He laughed a little and drank. 'I am not as young and handsome as you, Kolya.'

'Pah,' I said, waving him off. 'I don't have time for that.'

Papa sighed. 'Will I never have grandchildren?'

'Listen, all the world needs is more of us.' I didn't mean to be irritable, but he asks too much. I constantly disappoint him.

'I brought you something.' Papa reached behind and

picked up the parcel from the pillow.

I opened the bag and looked in. It was a small book on jade. The covers and pages were slick: inside were black and white photographs, and in the middle, four pages of color plates. 'It's beautiful, Papa.' I sat and sipped my vodka, looking at each piece illustrated. *It* wasn't in this book, either, but Papa knew that. He would buy me every book until we either found it, or were satisfied that we would never glimpse it again, even in a photo.

I went to the kitchen and brought the bottle back. Papa was resigned, he lifted his glass for more. 'Do you want to stay tonight?' I asked, feeling glad to have him with me after all.

'Yes, Nicholas, I think I should.'

And the seriousness of his face frightened me. He had brought news – Grandmama? I pulled a cigarette from my shirt pocket and lit it with a book of matches that lay on the floor.

'What?' I said impatiently.

'There is a man looking for us.'

'Oh.' I pulled in a breath of air, I don't know how. My chest felt crushed. 'Who?'

'A psychiatrist, I guess. He called Mama and talked to her.' Papa took another long drink. 'She didn't tell him anything. He didn't talk to her long, but he asked if he could visit her and she . . . '

'Wait, don't tell me anything for a minute.' I reeled when I stood. I hurried to the bathroom and stood over the john and heaved into it. I felt better, but still sick. I washed my face and hands. When I looked in the mirror, Papa was there, outside the bathroom.

'I'm sorry, Kolya.'

'Pour me another.'

'You still have some.'

I returned to the mattresses and stretched out. Suddenly, I was cold. Papa put my jacket over me.

'You see, he was clever. She's afraid she may have said the wrong things. He wants to visit her.'

'No, not Grandmama. She's as clever as he is, I'm sure,' I said. I pictured her in her chair, and this man (all I could see was a navy blue suit and a conservative tie) on the sofa. She would be doing needlework, and drinking a glass of hot tea.

'You're probably right,' Papa agreed. 'She worries more and more as she gets older. She said that the man wasn't sure who he was looking for – the Dal family, but she said she knew no other Dals, that she had never heard of Mikhail Nicholaevich.'

'He knew about Mikhail?' I said.

'Yes, Kolya.'

I wanted to get up and be sick again, but I lay still. I stared at the ceiling for a long while, and soon the sky went dark and also my apartment, and I fell asleep. When I woke the next morning, my father was trying to leave quietly. I didn't open my eyes to say goodbye to him.

23 February

I must do better. I realized today that my studies have been sinking. Have missed too many classes in past weeks. Well, I attended most of them, but I slept through one and a half last week. I think my literature professor has had enough of me; perhaps it was an over-sensitivity that made me take personally his comments on alcoholism. He was talking about writers when he said, 'Not a pretty sight.' And someone in class looked at me. I've also lost money by taking a day off from work at the library.

We are already talking about the end of the Wars of the Roses in English history; I don't remember much about the middle Plantagenets.

Richard the Third came up today. Of course, there was controversy. Dr Estes paced back and forth (oh, today she was gorgeous in corduroy, how I wish I could touch her) and I could sense that she liked having her students argue.

Anti-Richard: that pasty fellow who nearly wet his pants when Dr Park said a kind word about Mao in Far Eastern Civ. last semester. He is consistently anti-royalty, anti-government, so no surprise there.

Pro-Richard: Jack, the Jack who got her grade changed on the first exam when Dr Estes realized that Jack is a woman. At least, that is my suspicion of what they talked over that time after class. A preppie sort, though casual, she dresses in jeans, oxford shirts and loafers. I was surprised to see her being so emotional about something in class. But as soon as Dr Estes mentioned Richard, I looked over at Jack because I felt her snap. She sits right across the aisle from me, has borrowed pens, and once picked up a book I dropped.

Idealists, both of them, but I have to admit that I can smell the blood when I look at a painting of Richard. And his big brother, Edward! Did they really have faces like that then?

Here's what happened. Dr Estes was speaking in her soft voice, it was sunny and the windows were open. I was rolling my pencil under my palm, idly attempting to stay awake.

' . . . the traditional history is that Richard had his two nephews murdered, thereby making his way clear to the crown . . . '

That's when Jack seemed to jerk, and I felt that she was distressed. Strange, when I looked at her, I noticed for the first time that she had grey hairs in her black ones, and I focused on that for a moment. I have been attracted at times during the semester to her, but she is beyond me in so many ways that I let those feelings pass.

'But Shakespeare, Sir Thomas More, and others in the Tudor era did have an interest in making him a villain . . . ' Dr Estes went on.

The Maoist raised his hand here, and Dr Estes nodded to him. 'But, he probably *did* it. All this garbage about him being a good guy is just romantic bullcrap.'

'Oh, not really!' Jack said, and she looked a little

surprised herself that she'd spoken up like that. 'Have you read a book called *The Daughter of Time*? It's a detective novel that proves Richard couldn't have done it.'

A detective novel? The woman had courage, but still it was like admitting that you only know of literature from television plays. I was amazed that anyone would say such a thing. Well, that *Jack* would say such a thing, because I had thought her more sophisticated than that. And then she didn't even seem embarrassed about it. I was; I was terribly embarrassed for her.

Another student said, 'It's hard to improve your reputation when Shakespeare and a saint write nasty things about you.'

So, everyone seemed to know about Richard but me. I had been slow in reading the text. I felt left out of the argument, though I never say anything in class anyway. I have yet to raise my hand.

'But it was Morton,' Jack said knowingly. 'Bishop Morton wrote it, More just transcribed it, and they *thought* he wrote it. He was just a boy when Richard died.'

'So what?' said a faint voice from the other side of the room. Another giggled. I felt sorry for Jack, but obviously she knew what she was talking about.

'And history has just been carrying it on for centuries.' Jack looked at Dr Estes and her voice was a little quieter. 'I read a book that had changed Richard's motto to make him sound more mercenary. Can't remember what the motto was, about loyalty or something, and they changed it to make him sound power-hungry. And this was a real history book, warping the words that Richard lived by, not even checking up on it.'

I hadn't cared a whit about Richard the Third until this afternoon. I had hardly paid much attention to him other than as a fictional character in a play. In fact, I'd never read that one – only seen Olivier's version on the public broadcast station years ago.

Poor, sick Richard must have been mad to murder his nephews, and I felt this conviction as if someone who really knew was whispering through time into my ear – guilty, guilty, guilty.

Oh, it doesn't matter now, does it? Who cares? Jack does, and a few other buffs, but the screams of the children are so long past . . .

I don't know why I am even thinking about this. I don't want to.

Perhaps I am thinking about Jack. Felt something in her today. Something strong and lost, and it was like waking up confused after a long sleep. I have been thinking only of myself too much lately. Again.

27 February

English history class again, much quieter today. Dr Estes ticked off dates on the blackboard with a nub of chalk. Richard is in our past again. Now we start on the oddly disquieting Tudors, and I miss the Plantagenets. It seems that the fun is missing from Henry, sickly Edward, Mary, and even to a certain extent Elizabeth. How can the Armada compare with the Crusades? Or Sir Francis Drake with Robin Hood? No more Lionhearts, Lacklands, or Eleanors.

I wish I had been sober the past few weeks. I think I missed something important, and can't quite figure it out.

It's all important. I have to remember the time that I first told Grandmama that I was going away to college. She hated that, but I promised her (and myself) that I would make her proud.

I remember that she stood at the window, rubbing a wet circle in the frost and looking out at the snow. It was a good spring blizzard in the Rockies. That's when she told me that particular story about Mikhail. But at first, she just said 'away?' as if that had been the only word I'd said. 'Away, Kolya?'

I told her that I didn't want to work in a factory all my

life. I wanted to do something else, such as teaching, something quiet and bookish.

She said, 'When it snows like this in Denver, I miss the old house. At home, the family didn't leave. The old never had to live alone.'

I wanted to go away, yes, not because I didn't love her, but because I loved myself most of all. I couldn't stay. When I got up from the chair she knew what I was doing and told me not to get a drink.

'I want you to feel what I am feeling,' she had said, looking away from the winter outside. 'I want you to understand what it's like to be left behind. Come closer and listen to what I feel!'

I hadn't been able to move. She immobilized me with her anger.

I told her that the university had accepted me, they were going to give me money, and a student job in the library, and it was all planned. I reminded her that we had discussed it long ago.

'I'll call you. I'll visit. It's only a few hours away.'

'That's what your father said when he left. And he lives right here in Denver. You ever see my Sasha here for dinner, even on Sunday? No.'

'I'll be better,' I promised.

'Why can't you go to school here?'

'Because it isn't what I want.'

'You're a boy, Kolya.'

'No, I'm not. This is America, and I'm a man now. Just because I don't have a farm and a wife doesn't mean that I'm not grown up.'

She laughed at me. How long ago it seems now that she laughed at me, and I was so young that it still hurt for Grandmama to think me foolish. Then she stared out the window again. I remember how cold it was that day; the snow spat out of the sky, hard and bitter.

Nicholas Alexandrovich,' she said.

'What?'

'I'm afraid for you.'

'Why?'

'Because you . . . sometimes . . . you're so much like Mikhail. You're so lonely and brooding and you drink too much. Mikhail wasn't a bad man. The sensitivity ate at him more than the others. He *thought* about what he knew of others' feelings instead of just brushing them off, like the others did. I remember that he used to hide Jews in the barn. I don't know how they knew to come to him, but he always took them in. Nicholas Pavlovich chased them out sometimes if he saw them, but he didn't always look, even if he suspected they were there. Mikhail would take a chicken to the rabbis to be freshly killed, help them make their beds in the straw.'

I was surprised to hear Grandmama speak nicely of Mikhail. It was like a heresy. No one talked about him when Grandfather was alive. My father had told me about my great-uncle on a camping trip. Later, I realized that it was planned for the telling of family secrets – under the pines, next to a cold Colorado stream. I was only about five years old. My father told me about us.

'Imagine, Kolya, if very few men could smell. Only you, or your family, could smell all of the many things in this world. You would sometimes smell roses, and sometimes dung. But, just because you are the only one that is smelling them doesn't mean the odor belongs to you. People will give you their emotions without knowing it; remember that you are not them, that they don't know that you know. Do not confuse yourself with the other people around you.'

He told me about the fire in the head. I had no real idea of what he was talking about. Thinking back on it, I wonder if Papa ever knew the fire himself. He was so mild, but he built boundaries, something I never learned to do. Something most of the family never learned to do; my Papa was different. It took me a long time to understand what happens to us around other people – that day I was much more excited about catching a rainbow trout than hearing awful tales about dead relatives.

I was used to hearing stories about life in Russia. Some

are interesting, and I wish I had tape recordings now of my grandfather telling them. Grandfather's Uncle Vanya died while working on the Trans-Siberian Railway. Some say he fell and broke his neck, but a friend of the family told my great-great-grandfather that he had starved to death because he drank rather than spend all his pay on the three bowls of thin cabbage soup they served to the workers. The cabbage was usually rotten.

And there was a cousin who fought in the Great War. He had wandered out in the woods for a breather from his troop and encountered a German soldier, lost, and more frightened of the Russian winter than the enemy. The cousin traded his boots for the German soldier's gun, shot the German after the trade and took his boots back. That's how wars are won.

They talked of bad winters and eating famine bread; they talked of good harvests and prosperous times. They remembered little things and kept some of the culture alive in our house, which was a quiet, isolated bit of the old world in the middle of Denver, Colorado.

As I grew older, there was one person I became more interested in, whom I could never ask about. His name was never mentioned until after my grandfather died. Now I had this chance to question my grandmother. 'Did you know him well?' I asked her.

She smiled. 'I was so young, then. Only seventeen when I was a bride.'

'Did you like him?'

'Oh, yes. He was like a real brother to me. And Fyodor loved him, too.' Grandmama sat down on the sofa, remembering. 'Just before your grandfather died, he spoke of Mikhail. Once he caught an old tramp stealing eggs. Then the tramp picked up a shovel and hit Mikhail on the shoulder with it. It hurt him so badly that he couldn't use his arm for weeks, but the old tramp saw that Mikhail was just a lad and he dropped the shovel. Mikhail told him to take the eggs, and gave him a loaf of bread and some apples, too.'

I asked her why.

'Mikhail was like that. He then gave him a candle. It was a sort of joke somehow to Mikhail, because he said the candle was smarter than the tramp at finding the way in the dark. Just before Fyodor died, he said maybe he would meet his brother in heaven and maybe . . . '

I remember finishing the sentence for her. She had gotten old and, like old widows, she cried easily. So I said, 'Maybe Mikhail would be waiting with his candle.'

Why am I thinking of such melancholy things today?

2 March

It's snowing.

I stopped at the liquor store and the clerk with the rocky, athletic face was working behind the counter. How I hate him! He sees me too clearly. I used to think that he had the Dal sensitivity, but I could never feel it. I have stopped searching for others like me anyway, but he just seemed to see right through me. He's ugly inside, so smug and sure that I am an alcoholic. He smells foreignness on me, and once asked me where I was from. When I told him that I was born in St Luke's Hospital in Denver, he just said, 'huh,' and never spoke to me personally again.

I am sitting by my window, looking at the snow piling up on the railing. The weather was warm until last evening, then the clouds came in over the mountains. This is heavy, wet snow. There are three inches of it sitting on the railing, but it is already melting, soaking into the splintered wood. I wonder if I should offer to paint this old house for the landlady.

Feeling lonely. Not much to say.

4 March

Sunday. I worked in the library this afternoon, trying to make up some of the time I had missed. A lot happened because of this and it's very late at night right now. I can't sleep though.

Was reading about Henry's wives, trying to catch up – Catherine of Aragon, Mary's mother; Anne Boleyn, Elizabeth's; and Jane Seymour, Edward's. Then no more children for the old goat.

I looked up. The library was busy for a Sunday. Organized students are already getting ready for term papers, midterms. Stacks of books at their elbows, fingers flying over indexes, searching out key words, picking through the card catalogs.

I noticed someone, sitting on the carpet by one of the stacks, one knee drawn up, a book settled on her thigh, concentrating.

It was my classmate, Mad Jack, the one having the posthumous affair with Richard the Third. I have been thinking of her since she unknowingly revealed so much of herself last week. I didn't like to, but I couldn't help but watch her. It was so hopeless to want her. Her hand scooted down the page as she read. She was oblivious to the world. What I would give for that peace of mind! Ornette, the other work-study student behind me, was in a rage about her boyfriend, and I was oppressed by that. I could hardly read at all until I'd gone to the john and had a drink. Then, I was sleepy.

I felt sorry for myself, watching Jack read. Here I am, twenty-seven years old, barely scraping by with a 'C' average, just a senior. There was Jack, perhaps twenty-one, the kind of kid on the Dean's list, probably a junior.

It makes me want to work especially hard to see punk faces getting ahead. I tried to read about Henry's effect on the Church. I found myself daydreaming about another book I wanted to read instead.

'Hi.'

I was glad I'd fortified myself with that little nip because Jack stood there in front of me, radiating friendliness. I checked her books, glanced at her ID, and figured she was going to do her term paper on Guess Who.

'Have you dropped English history class?' she asked.

'No.' She hadn't seen me slinking into the back row, late. 'Changed seats so I could get more sleep.'

She laughed. 'Well, I think it's an interesting class myself.' She watched me stamp her books. 'I can't remember your name.'

'Nicholas Dal,' I said, pushing her books at her. I got the blood of tyrants on my hands, touching her books. I felt her looking at me. I saw her trying not to smile. I wanted her to go away because she distracted me in the most basic way.

'My name is Jack Berdo.'

I happened to look at her ID again. 'That's not what your card says.' I had always suspected her name to be Jacqueline or some such, but it said Susanne Elizabeth Berdo. This had escaped me on first glance because I wanted to hurry her. But now it was something to chat about.

'Family joke,' she said simply, and put her card back into her book bag. 'What kind of accent is it that you have?'

'Russian.'

She liked that. I was doing all right. 'When did you come here?' she asked.

'A very long time ago. Before you were born.'

'I see.'

I regretted the deception immediately, but didn't want to explain it away. It didn't matter. Of all people, I had expected she might spot the apple pie American in me. No, she was so *adjusted* that she would be the first to spot the bortsch on my chin. She would never go out with me, would she, I wondered? But, she seemed interested. She wanted to talk to me.

'You read very quickly,' I said.

'What?'

'I was watching you.' I pointed to the spot where she had been sitting. 'You read so quickly.'

'Oh. Maybe so.' She blushed a little. 'I like to read.'

'Yes, so do I, but I can never read well in public places.'

She nodded, understanding in her way. We smiled at each other. 'Why are you called Jack then?' I asked, curious.

'My mother's name is Susanne, too, and my father just called me that from the time I was a baby so he wouldn't get us mixed up.'

I felt something odd happening to her, as if she were dissolving into the floor. Her face began to change, to droop with worry or depression. It revolved around the word mother, I think. She is more complex that I had given her credit for, and I wanted to reach over and take her arm to keep her from disappearing. She was suddenly no longer *there*, with me, but was staring at the carpet.

'So, Jack it has been all your life,' I said. 'Yes, Jack?'

She returned in a flickering. She nodded. 'Well, I tried Susanne out when I was younger, but it just isn't me.'

'Why don't we have coffee together sometime?' I suggested.

She raised her eyebrows. 'Sure, I'd like to.' The world brightened.

What? I was surprised at how pleasantly she accepted. 'This evening?' I pressed, thinking that anything was possible.

'All right.'

'I finish work at five. We can meet . . . '

'Oh, I'll just hang around.' I noticed that her hands were trembling just as much as mine as she slid her books off the counter. 'Is that all right?'

'Yes!' I said. 'But it's only three-thirty.'

'Then I won't have to read so fast,' she replied, walking away. She disappeared in the stacks where I could no longer see her.

What have I done, I thought? I always think that I need this kind of thing until it happens. Oh, yes, I have the urges, and I have them often and powerfully, but to invite someone to be close to me always means disaster. I already see the illusions bursting one by one from my mind and her mind; I see myself clawing my way out and away. To ask someone to assume they might grow close to me is a cruelty I can't seem to keep myself from performing time after time.

Even I get lonely, though. Even I crave a sigh, a kiss, a bit of affection. And even I can pretend to care in return, as long as I can go away and breathe every now and then.

Don't ask for more. I'm cold inside because I've felt it all. I'm only interested in what is real to me, and the most authentic feeling I ever have is to be left in peace.

Poor Jack. She's a good kid.

I left Ornette at the desk while I took a break to have a cigarette and a little more vodka from my pocket flask. The warm day hadn't yet melted the most stubborn snow. The sky was bright blue, the drainpipes were gurgling and cars slushed through filthy streets. The mountains are beautiful on days like this – cold and clear, so close. The sun marked out the textures in the jagged rock and a few solitary pines.

At two minutes to five, Jack wandered back to the desk. I had wondered if she would change her mind and slip out somehow, but there she was. She only looked up casually from beside the security gate as I gathered my books and put on my jacket.

'Would you like something to eat?' I asked her, outside.

'I guess I'm a little hungry,' she said.

'I know a place with good Mexican food. All right?' Then I remembered my bicycle. 'It's in walking distance, if you don't mind a walk.'

'I have my truck,' she said.

We decided to put my bicycle in the back of her truck and drive, since it was already dark. I got in the truck and pulled out a cigarette.

'You aren't going to light that in here, are you?' she said.

'Of course not.' I held it, as if that's all I had intended to do. When we arrived, I got out of the truck and tried to light my smoke in the breeze. I thought it might be handsome, Bogartish, but Jack stood on the sidewalk with her hands in her coat pockets, walking back and forth in front of the tavern door. I got it lit and we went inside.

I was no longer hungry. In fact, I'd had enough to drink that drinking was what I cared most about. She ordered a green chili burrito (why are they little burros, I wondered?). I ordered a bowl of chili. And the usual. This bartender knows me and gave me a water glass three-quarters filled. 'The Russian,' he always says, laughing, giving me my drink.

Jack looked at my drink, surprised. She thought it water, I think, until she saw the way I sipped at it. She was too perceptive, too smart and too proper for me. I felt under glass with her and wanted to get the evening over painlessly. I drank my vodka in a gloom of insecurity as she stared around the tavern.

'Well,' she said, 'what are you studying?'

'History, but eventually I'm going for a Master's in library science.'

'Oh. Library science?' She seemed interested. 'I've never known anyone who actually wanted to be a librarian. I guess it would be fun, working with books all day.'

'If that's what a librarian does. Actually, it's a lot of detailed, cataloging work. Has to be one of the dullest graduate programs. I'm sure I'll like it, though.' I lit another cigarette. I was feeling safer with her – it was always a good idea to talk about school, it got conversations going. 'And you?'

'Anthropology.'

'Another useful social science, like history. The world is clamoring for more of us.' I was glad to hear it, though. She nodded.

There was another silence. She said suddenly, 'Are you called Nick?', as if she had been wondering and had just found the nerve to ask.

'Kolya.'

'Kolya?' She smiled. 'That's exotic.'

The talk faltered again. We both looked around at others in the tavern.

I shrugged, not sure what to say next. She has deep brown eyes. Grandmama's must have been that dark when she was young. The Dals have grey ones, like mine, and I like looking at Jack's brown eyes.

'What's your whole name?' she asked.

'Nicholas Alexandrovich.'

'So, that means your father was named Alexander?'

'Yes. He is Alexand – well, Sasha. Like Kolya for Nicholas.' I regretted again having been evasive earlier, when it hadn't seemed important to make things clear. How would I say outright that I had given her a wrong impression? 'What's your father's name?' I asked.

'Paul.'

'Susanna Pavlovna,' I told her.

'Doesn't sound a bit like me,' she said, dismissing it.

The food came and we concentrated on eating. I forced the chili down somehow. Truth is, I don't like Mexican food, but I like the tavern. Went to the bar, got her another beer and held out my water glass for a little more.

She thanked me for the beer; her burrito was hotter than she had bargained for and she had to wipe her nose a lot. Tears stood in her eyes as she ate, which seemed to embarrass her. She wouldn't look at me. 'Hot, hot,' she said, 'but good.'

I didn't really know what I wanted to do at that point. She could have walked out or gone home with me and it would have left me indifferent.

I didn't know what to say to Jack. Her moods shifted rapidly, and I felt pressed to distract her from some important pain. It was a lot of work just to sit with her.

As she wiped her fingers with the cloth napkin (everything is red there – the walls, the booths, the menus, the napkins) she said, 'Why did your family come to America?'

'Everyone wants to come to America,' I said, seeing my chance. 'Actually, I was born here.' There, now things had been put right.

'Oh. What about your accent?'

'We speak Russian at home. I suppose it's the same as a

23

family one generation from Mexico. I don't think of myself as having an accent, though.'

'Well, you do. Which language do you think in?'

It stopped me. No one has ever asked me that. My thoughts are so unlike speaking that I had never considered it concretely. 'I suppose in Russian. I write notes to myself in it.'

'Oh.' She stared at me quietly, a glint of interest shining in her eyes. I relaxed. She was approving somehow, not as scrutinizing. I can't live up to the approval, but I smiled at her.

'Have you ever been to the Soviet Union?' she asked.

'God, no!'

'Oh, that answers that, doesn't it?' She laughed. 'I would love to go. In fact, I'm saving money for a trip to Europe. My father is going to help. Maybe next summer.'

'Europe?' I said. 'I don't have much interest in travel myself.'

She fell into an introspective silence. 'I hope I can go,' she finally said.

'Why wouldn't you?'

'Lots of reasons.' Now it was her turn to be evasive. The *something* I had detected in the library was back. She had a burning wound in her, and it was fresh. Even drunk, I could see it. Her eyes sank, her posture changed, her mouth was tight. She took another drink of her beer.

'That's not water you're drinking, is it?' she said. 'I thought it was at first.'

'No, it's not water.'

'You drink a lot?'

'I don't think so.'

'I'm sorry,' she said, sitting up straight. 'I don't know why I even said that. It's none of my business. I've just noticed the way you are in class sometimes . . . ' She made a flurry of gestures aiming toward an apology, but looking more like nervousness.

I finished my vodka. 'I hope that won't discourage you from coming up to my apartment for coffee.'

She raised her eyebrows slightly. 'I don't know.'

'We can just talk if you like.' I swear that I meant it at that moment. I just wanted to have her company a little longer. I was intrigued by her secrets. I wanted to look at her a little longer.

'Well, all right.'

When we got up to leave, I felt a little unsteady. But I managed to pay the ticket. Jack left a tip. I followed her out to her truck. We'd forgotten to lock up my bicycle, but it was still there. A thief wouldn't believe such an obvious prize as a ten-speed in the back of a truck, ready to be ridden away, so it had been unmolested. I rolled the window of the truck down, feeling rather closed in.

Jack is a wonderful driver – so confident. Her truck is a small make. Watching her feet working the clutch and accelerator, her hand working the shift expertly, made me feel even drunker. I should have tried to stay a little more sober, I could have studied her, but I still watched her closely.

'Nice to be so near to school,' she said, after I'd given directions.

'Where do you live?' I asked.

'Across town. I still live with my parents.'

'You mean that you grew up in this town? I thought all the students here had come from somewhere else, and the children from here went away to Denver or Boston or whatever to go to school.'

'No, I grew up here. I couldn't afford to live anywhere except at home. Well, and save the money to go to Europe. I want to stay all summer. I want to follow the amber trade route, dig through things, get my hands in some kitchen middens, stuff like that. Besides, I don't mind my family. I don't do much that they say anything about. Stay in my room and read.'

Uh-oh, not a virgin, I was thinking. But I was not a virgin and I would describe my life as sitting in my room reading, too. I worried a little. I remembered that I had no wine or anything for her to drink with me later on. And it was Sunday – no chance to buy anything. I directed her down the alley to a parking place. She followed as I walked my bicycle in to the yard. The landlady's lights were off; the house would be quiet. Though the woman downstairs hardly interfered, I always preferred her to be sleeping or gone when I had company.

Jack picked up her book bag. She looked apprehensive. If she had only known that she was entering the den of a fool maniac, she would have looked even more nervous. God, I wished I hadn't drunk so much! I wished that I could open her up and read her straight out, and have all that done with, but that would be to my advantage. And she still, slowly, would have to learn all about me.

Learn to despise me. Or feel indifference. This is what happens.

I say this as if I want her to be with me for a long while, but I don't think there's much chance of that.

Through her, I saw my yard anew – flaking paint, brown patchy lawn, spare tires leaning against the garage, plastic garbage bags soggy with melting snow, the sagging reed fence.

'Jack,' I said, feeling a fright, feeling that I needed to give her a chance to back out. Her expression worried me. 'I must warn you . . . '

She gave me a glance. 'What's that?' But her voice was only curious, not alarmed.

'I don't believe in Richard the Third's innocence.'

She laughed. 'Well, we can talk about that.'

Her good nature made me lust after her. We went up the stairs. I paused, feeling out of my apartment for intruders, but no one was there. I opened the door. No one had entered while I was gone, at least, not that I could detect. I looked in the closet at my diary and letter box, and then turned to Jack. 'Would you like coffee?'

'Yes, sounds good.'

I didn't remember leaving that cup on the sink before I left, but yes, that was from this morning. I made the coffee. I like the sound of my electric coffee maker. It's always a comfort on cold mornings, and with company, it sounds festive. It was strange to have someone walking around in the apartment, looking at my books and things.

I took her jacket and hung it over the back of my desk chair. I invited her to sit, but there is only that one chair. She sat down on the edge of the mattresses, her eyes still checking the book titles from where she sat.

Our feet were wet and I saw the shiny footprints on the linoleum in the hallway.

'Well, not a fancy place,' I said. I am always critical of it when I bring someone home, but I actually like it.

'It's nice. I wish I had a place of my own.'

'I thought you liked living with your parents.'

'Well, you know . . . It would be better *not* to.'

I thought of Grandmama, but said nothing. I made a resolve to call Grandmama in the morning because I hadn't talked to her for over a week. 'Are you warm enough?' I asked.

'Oh, yeah, I'm fine.' She wore a sweater and jeans. Her maroon sweater was dark in the dim light. I looked at her hair.

I was nervous. Wanted to get another drink. Wanted to go outside and get a breath of cold air to sober up. Wanted her. I lit a cigarette.

'That's a nasty habit,' she said.

'Yes, I know. I like it though. My father smokes cigars sometimes. That's worse.'

'I guess so.'

What is she thinking? She was watching me so tentatively. 'You read a lot,' she said.

'Yes.'

She stood, perhaps as restless as myself, and walked to the bookcase. 'What's this? All jade?'

'Oh, jade,' I said, feeling less and less coherent the longer she was in the room with me. I struggled to carry on a conversation. I was wearing out. 'I collect.' I now smoked the cigarette furiously. It had a long orange cinder on one end.

She touched my jade, rubbing the Buddha's belly. It didn't matter that I stood there, she was entertaining herself.

'Coffee's ready.' I poured two cups, and started to whiten hers, when I remembered that I hadn't asked. 'Milk?' I said.

'What?'

'Milk?' I said again.

'Sorry.' She came to the kitchen door. 'What?'

'Milk . . . ' I repeated, then realized that I'd said *moloko*, not milk, which I had meant to say. '*Milk?*'

'No, just a little sugar.'

I sprinkled it on. As I handed the cup to her, I saw something which frightened me. It was a flame, leaping across the surface of her coffee. I jumped, spilled some of the coffee on my hand. Then I realized that it was only the reflection of the light bulb.

It was a silly reaction. Why hadn't I ever noticed that before? Jack scrutinized me. 'Are you okay?'

'Yes, yes. I thought I˙ saw an ant in your coffee. Sometimes I have ants here.'

'We do, too,' she said as we walked into the other room. 'They like the dog food.'

'You have a dog?'

'We used to. He was my mother's dog.'

'The elder Susanne.'

Jack gave me a look. I didn't understand it. We sat down. She looked into her coffee.

I saw the flame again. Did she see it, too? Or was it just my memory of the flame? No light bulbs above us in the living room. 'Jack, give me your cup.'

Obediently, she handed it over. Her coffee was hotter than mine, and the flame was still there. It had a face. 'Not that,' I said. I dumped the coffee into the kitchen sink, poured and sugared another for her. That cup was all right. My hands were trembling.

Something was going wrong. It was Jack. She brought it with her. I opened the cupboard door to find my vodka.

Jack stood at the kitchen door. 'What the hell are you doing? Trying to get me drunk?'

'No, that isn't it. It was for me.'

'Chrissakes,' she said, 'you aren't a virgin, are you?'

I stared at her. That was funny. The flames were gone now; Jack was funny and I wanted her. I laughed, and that made her laugh, too. I said, 'no,' in case she suspected my laughter was a cover-up. A barrier was passed. We were no longer strangers struggling to say things to thread the time together.

'I hope I don't worry you too much,' I said. 'I really am relatively harmless.'

'No, you don't worry me,' she replied. 'You do surprise me, though.'

'How am I surprising?'

'Well, I thought that you were from somewhere else all this time, until this evening. You get words confused, and you seem so . . . how do I explain it? . . . interested in what I'm saying, as if it's all new to you. The way people are when they are genuinely working to understand.'

'Yes,' I nodded. She didn't know that she was talking to a mirror with a soul, however dark. I couldn't help but be interested in others as long as they enjoyed hearing themselves.

'I suppose Americans are too homogenous anyway,' she said. 'I realize how much like everyone else I must seem to you because you are different, and yet we grew up less than a hundred miles apart. Why should it be like that?'

'Well, I wish I were more ordinary.' I felt this to be true at that moment, though sometimes I cherish my differences.

'I like your foreignness, even if you are an American,' she said as we settled on the mattresses, cups in hand. 'I suppose that's the anthropologist in me.'

'I want to be *more* American,' I confessed.

'But, why? What's wrong with the way you are? You're unique.'

'But, no, you don't understand. I am the same inside, no

matter what I sound like. The accent is like clothing. Take it off and there are my words, naked.'

She smiled.

'You see, I don't even know what to do. I don't listen to myself. If you hear me say something that sounds different, tell me.'

'Oh, I don't know if I want to. You're so charming.'

She meant this. I was pleased, but still wanted to make her understand. 'Well, that charm is not very deep,' I said.

'All right, I'll tell you. But this is going to be a lot of work, because you say things differently all the time.'

'Such as?'

'Well, *that* sounded all right. Let's see. First, it's your "r," then. When you say an "r," it sounds different, like you roll up your tongue or something.'

We practiced with that sound for a while. Jack grinned the whole time. She was having fun with me. I finally began to feel her sounds in my mouth, duplicating her accent as she said words. We got a book out and I read every word with an 'r' for a couple of pages. When I got to the word 'fruit,' she collapsed in a giggling fit.

'What?' I asked. 'What's so funny?'

'Oh,' she gasped, 'I'm sorry.'

At first, I was embarrassed at the way she laughed at me. But she was so tickled that I couldn't help but join her. We got over it, but then when I repeated the word, she began again.

Our arms touched. I was overwhelmed with passion for her. She was so soft, so sweet, so happy, lying back on my bed, laughing. I leaned over her and kissed her.

Such a nice kiss it was, too. So soft, so responsive, so affectionate. I wanted to explore her completely. I wanted her badly. She looked at me seriously after the kiss.

'Fruit,' I said, wanting her to smile again.

She did. 'You just say the "u" – not "froo-it" but "froot," uhm, like "toot." ' All this she said softly, watching me.

'Froot,' I said.

'You sound like an American, Kolya.'

'I am an American. I belong here as much as you.'

'Then you should be called Nick.'

'Too Hemingway.'

'You're so bookish. You should have learned to play football instead of reading books.'

I smiled at her, and stroked her forehead with my thumb. Her hair was tangled in my fingers.

'But then,' she said, 'if you weren't bookish, I wouldn't be here.'

'You like that, do you?' I asked.

'Yes.'

I kissed her again.

We undressed each other slowly, touching. Then, we made love greedily, as if it had been a long time for both of us. It had for me. I covered us with a blanket and put one arm across her middle, and the other above her head and watched her fall asleep. Eventually, I slept, too.

I should have known better than to sleep with Jack there. First came the dreams, then the fever. The dreams were strange and disguised, unmemorable in waking, but they started the fever. Jack roused because I had pulled the blanket off her and was shivering under it.

'What's this, delirium tremens?' she asked, half-asleep, but as much awake.

The sand shifted in my brain. I ached. I told Jack that she had better go, but to no use because I couldn't remember how to say it in her language. My heart pounded.

She touched me. A cool palm on my chest was like salve. She invaded me. She was so close that she was swallowing me. I could only feel her desire for me. Or was it mine for her? I didn't know, but I tried to move toward her.

'You're so hot. Are you sick?' she asked softly.

'No, I'm hot.' I touched her breast. She spread her cold hands all over me, and discovered what she wanted to find. Then she sat on me. She was still damp.

It was more than greed this time. I felt the fever

subsiding, my head growing lighter, but still she was there in me and I was in her and I'd never experienced anything like it.

It is the first time I have ever made love to a woman while sober.

Technically.

Such a painful sort of pleasure it was – I wanted it to happen, and yet never to end. I was insatiable as it happened. I discovered all her places and every time I found something new to please her I was awash with her pleasure. I had the whole thing occurring in me twice, within the same time and place.

I didn't know where she ended and I began and didn't care. We were slick with sweat, earnest, and we pushed each other off at the same moment. I went blind and deaf, but not insensible.

Then, a silence containing only breathing.

'Damn,' she said, amazed.

I laughed.

In the haze of afterwards, I had forgotten how I'd felt just a few moments before. It had happened quickly, and been over, just like the sex. Now I was calmer.

That's what I thought.

Jack lay beside me, slowly moving her hand across my belly. I looked at her and smiled. But she didn't look at me. She didn't smile.

Something began to squirm within me again. It was going to come back. I dreaded it.

'Where's your phone?' she asked, peering at the clock face beside me.

'I don't have one.'

'I have to go.'

'No, wait. Yes, you'd better go, I see.' I knew I sounded confused. 'I'll . . . . ' But I couldn't imagine what the rest of that sentence might have been. She was confusing the hell out of me.

Horror came into me. I watched her dress, and didn't want her to leave. I grieved to see her go and leave me alone. I was terrified that I'd done something wrong and that she was angry.

'Jack.'

'It's all right. I'm sorry to run, but I have to go. I'll see you in class.' She jangled her keys, standing aside in the shadows, looking at me (I guessed).

I stood, pulled my jeans on, and walked with her to the door. She kissed me and ran down the steps and across the yard. She got into the truck. The red tail lights came on, a wake of pebbles and gravel flew as she drove away.

Then it was a relief to be alone again.

5 March

I didn't see Jack on campus today. Went to work. Was sober all day. Stayed up late to do homework.

It was peaceful.

Dammit.

I like to be alone, I do.

Jack has death-feelings in her. Why?

Has she been sent to find me? Is she from them?

Oh, no, I mustn't think these things. I must remember that I am only myself, I am not important. The man is looking for me (he wants *me*, though, not my father) not because I am more sensitive and on the records, but because I am on the records, and I am a heftier prize.

Oh, I wish I had never been young. I wish that I had never been. I wish that I had been born the rock-jawed kid in the liquor store.

Why does Jack know death?

Why has she brought death to sit in me like this?

I am going to get a drink.

It will happen to *me*. Some day I'll cease. No more. My heart will stop, my blood will pool according to gravity, my brain will lose its electricity and my eyes will be fixed. That is not frightening because it is nothing.

The fear is in *knowing*.

I scrape and claw to stay alive. I feel myself sucked to the other side and I bury my fingers into what life I can hold on to, and death tugs. There is always one more thing to do, another thing to put right, another moment to live. What will they remember of me fifty years from now? Nothing? Wait, give me one more second, one more hour, one more day.

I NEVER WANT TO KNOW THAT I AM DYING!

And the time comes and closes your eyes and you know you're leaving . . .

I don't want to do it.

I think I'll live for ever, raping the heart of the world. I will go and consume every miserable soul, drink them dry, happy sad angry loving depressed sick ecstatic insane and then I'll keep going.

My God, I never thought sex would be like that. I want it again. I chased death from her for a few moments – she thought of me inside her, me looking at her face, my skin where it touched her, the sound of my voice . . . She thought of *me*, not death.

I hope she comes back.

I can stand the flames for a little while.

But I don't mind being alone. Really, I like it. It's better.

6 March

Thursday we have an exam in English history. Saw Jack today after class. I knew something was up. I slipped away to the men's room before we talked and took a little drink from my flask.

She was depressed. How incongruous – it was a pretty, blue, sunny day. We stood outside the Science building where my chemistry class was commencing while she told me her news. Her mother is ill; she has cancer and they got the results of a liver biopsy yesterday. The cancer has spread there from a bowel tumor. All the while a mild spring breeze blew in Jack's face and I stared again at those bright silver hairs in the sunlight, shining like tinsel.

I asked her if I could do anything to help. She shook her head and began to cry, turning her face toward the building. I felt protective and stood over her so that other students passing by couldn't spy on her moment.

She said she probably wouldn't be able to see me for a while, that the family was all sort of hanging together at the moment. 'My father,' she said, 'is pretending that nothing is happening.' She explained that he won't hear anything that might hint at how sick her mother is, that he talks about when she comes home from the hospital and gets better.

I didn't know what to say. I just listened to her.

After we parted I went into my chemistry class (late) and could hardly concentrate on what was being said. I thought about the fact that I should probably stay away from Jack. I can't take it. But then she says and does things that make me want to be with her.

'I'm glad I have you to talk to now,' she said.

When I got home, Gus came around to visit. He wanted to know if he could borrow my bicycle for the week while his brother-in-law was working on his car. I said sure, I didn't really need it since the weather was turning so nice, it would be a pleasant walk to school anyway. Gus had brought some beer, as he usually does, and we sat and drank and talked. Gus is having problems with Freda again. Same thing. I listened, and never made a single suggestion. I've learned to keep my mouth shut while Gus is talking about it. At the end of several hours, he punched me on the shoulder, told me I am a great friend, and left with my bicycle.

I was exhausted.

8 March

I got to class just as Dr Estes handed out the exam. My seat had been taken, so I had to sit at the back, where I couldn't see Jack's face. I could see her shoulders and the back of her head as she hunched over her paper, already working out the wonders of the Wars of the Roses. Most likely, Richard was riding his horse, off to save his little nephew King Edward from the greedy Woodvilles. Shit. I looked at the questions. I'm a history major, I should know this stuff.

I wanted to write down Li Po's line, 'I study antiquity to search for the ultimate essence . . . ' and add my notation to Dr Estes ' . . . and not details, details!' Would Li Po have test anxiety? Would his hands be wet? Would he be unable to read the questions? If I'd been in the China of Li Po's time, I wouldn't have had such a rough time of it. The world wasn't so skeptical. I would have been a mage, people would have traveled from afar to consult me.

I finally settled down and began to write.

Forty-five minutes later, Jack got up, handed her exam in, gathered her books and jacket, and passed me on her way out without even a glance. She looked tired, wrung out, but I resisted turning in my exam to follow her.

I don't care. To hell with women anyway. I don't need aggravation right now.

But when I put my exam on Dr Estes's desk, I thought of how I've had a desire for her for three semesters now, though a distant and respectful sort of desire. Dr Estes has probably been to England and touched the Tower of London, walked the streets where centuries of real but storybook characters have paraded. She's calm, intelligent, and perhaps a lot of fun drunk. Hey, Lenore, want to come up to my cozy little place sometime and discuss the great processes and movements of European history? Ah, no, I couldn't hold my ground against you for a moment. We could talk for a while and I could find a weak spot in you – everyone has one – and I could drag your dreams out on the rug and . . . no, I'd be drunk. You'd be disgusted. I'd pass out or vomit. Forget it. I'll be the student and you'll be the professor, and we'll overlook the fact that we graduated from high school the same year.

I fell asleep during chemistry again.

I went to work. Patricia, the circulation librarian, approached me with a note as soon as I came in the door. It had started raining while I was in class. This was a direct result of lending Gus my bicycle. I hoped he was riding across town and getting splashed by potato chip trucks. The library smelled of wet hair and coats, and muddy tracks darkened the path from the front door, fanning out into the library.

'Kolya,' Patricia said, 'I have an urgent message for you.' She stood close to me. Patricia wears a lot of perfume and I nearly choke when she gets that close. Patricia stands to my shoulder, wears billowy dresses and pointy little shoes, has a really good heart. 'I couldn't understand what she was saying very well, but she asked me to have you call her as soon as you came in.'

It was Grandmama. Something's happened to Papa, I thought.

'Thank you,' I said, and dove out the front doors again. I headed for the telephone booth. I never talk to family on phones with extension lines. Not that many people understand us.

The phone rang three times. Where is she? Hospital, police, where? 'Grandmama?'

'Oh, Kolya.' She sounded relieved to hear from me. It wasn't too awful, she wasn't tearful. 'There was a man. The man Sasha told you about. He came back, this time he was looking for Alexander or Nicholas or Fyodor. He has names now.'

'Who is he?'

'I don't remember his name. I couldn't understand some of what he said. He asked me about Mikhail again, and then asked me about Fyodor. He knows a little more now. I pretended not to understand him at all, so I wouldn't have to talk to him, but he spoke to me in Russian, too. I didn't tell him anything, Kolya, but he was sitting there with his notebook and your letter was on the table. He wrote down your address without asking me.'

'Who is he? What does he want?' I shouted.

'I don't know!' She began to cry.

I felt brutal for shouting. 'I'm sorry. I'm not angry with you. If he comes, I just won't talk to him, either. You did all right, I know you didn't do it on purpose.'

'I'm sorry, Kolya,' she said, still crying.

'I'll come to see you this weekend, okay? Don't cry. I'll see you on Sunday. How is that?'

She sounded calmer. 'Have you seen Sasha?'

'Not since the visit I told you about. He told me that you sent him that newspaper story. Listen, can you tell me what the man looks like?'

'He is small, dark-haired. Maybe he's a Jew. He looked forty, maybe less. I didn't hear his name, I was so nervous.'

'Is he an American?'

'I think so. He had a television accent.'

'Grandmama, next time he comes – maybe he won't – tell him that you're sick and can't see him, then call me just like you did today. You did everything just right.'

'Thank you, Kolya. I'm glad. Are you all right?'

I was shaken, but I wasn't going to admit that to her. 'Fine.'

'What would you like for dinner Sunday?'

'Anything. Anything you cook. Pot roast?'

She sighed. 'I'm sorry, Kolya,' she said again.

'It's all right, don't worry. I have to go to work now, but I'll see you in a few days.'

'Okay, goodbye.'

'Goodbye, I love you,' I said.

'Goodbye, I love you, too.' She hung up.

I glanced up and down the street, expecting to see this man somewhere nearby. No one but students, umbrellas, and myself, getting sprinkled on the head and shoulders as I stood by the phone.

I don't have to tell anyone anything any more. I have

learned this. How can anyone know unless we tell them? They'll never know. They'll never be able to take me again. I have learned. I just don't want to have to run. I've taken such a long time to get this far, and it has been so difficult . . . I don't want to run.

Maybe I should move, though. Time for another apartment. But will he be able to find me as long as I'm in town? And won't he suspect that I am a student at the university? I can't start all over again now. God, I'll be thirty soon and I don't want to end up like my father. If it gets too much, I can just lie low for a semester. No one will look that long. We can't be that important. He's probably a journalist, not a psychiatrist.

I'm not going to be paranoid about him.

Paranoid.

What an old and friendly word now. It masks the truth. It is *my* mask. It is definable, understandable, and even written about in books.

I had a dream a while ago, before I began to write here at my desk. It woke me with a jerk. It was the voice. And it was in my ear.

I sat up. The apartment was dark. The only real sound was that of the house settling, my refrigerator, and the wind blowing doors and fences and branches.

I know that I was awake, sitting up, when I heard his voice again.

'Nicholas Alexandrovich, take the candle.'

'I don't want your candle,' I said, and waited, but nothing happened.

10 March

Saturday at last. I had planned a beer with Gus sometime during the day, but it worked out differently. Early this morning, I got a newspaper. I sat on my bed, going through the rental ads with a red pen. There weren't many possibilities for a place – too expensive, too far away, too many people nearby, too near a hospital or church. I had liked this apartment until now.

I was doing this when I realized that my landlady had a visitor. I went to the window facing the street and looked out. It had been raining most of the morning. Everything was wet and shiny; cars gleamed, the grass looked especially green, the bark of the trees was a rich brown. And I could see the sun, small and grey, a diffuse spot halfway up the sky.

At first, I didn't see anyone. A strange car was parked at the curb. Then, I saw an umbrella coming out from under the porch downstairs. I couldn't really tell what kind of person was under the umbrella yet. Too distant. Papa is sensitive that far, but I was never good at long distances. The umbrella moved out, and I thought he was leaving, but then he turned and moved alongside the house, coming around to the back.

I jumped away from the window. I knew for certain who it was then. I *knew*. I was in a sweat, but shivering. I had to sit down as I felt him walking toward me.

Then I started to sense him. I became curious and excited, and I wanted to find . . . No, *I* am the prize. He was expecting to find something good here.

I heard his footsteps on the stairway, and I felt myself moving toward the door.

I am trembling, now, remembering it. I am remembering something else at the same time. They seem to be the same memory in feeling; though different in event.

My mother, Miranda, in defiance of the family, came to talk to my teacher after school one day. This was my fifth grade, before my grandfather died, which made Miranda's rebellion against the family that much worse.

She talked with the teacher about me as I sat at my desk. The teacher was surprised that Miranda was so ordinary – she had expected an old Slav in a babushka, I suppose, and instead was talking to a pretty, dark-haired woman, who had come with her parents from Minnesota during the

Depression. That was the extent of her being an immigrant.

On the other hand, my mother was surprised that my teacher had no complaints about me. 'I can't believe you haven't noticed that he's odd.'

I don't remember what I thought at that moment, but it was probably embarrassment that my mother would speak of family things to a stranger. How I was had nothing to do with my fifth-grade teacher.

'He doesn't even speak English at home. He doesn't speak to me.'

I was trying *not* to know how they were feeling. Blocking them out gave me a cramp in the back of my neck. I opened up my reader and looked at the pictures. A boy living in mid-America at the turn of the century played with dogs and hoops, rode an impossible bicycle, and waved to the engineer of a steam locomotive. He wore short trousers and a cap. I studied that with all my concentration, but I couldn't help but hear what they said about me.

My mother said, 'My husband doesn't listen to me when I say that Nicholas is not well adjusted. He and Nicholas are very close. The whole family is close. In fact, they're closed.' And her voice began to quiver.

My teacher shifted in her chair. She hadn't bargained for this kind of session. 'Sometimes immigrant families have trouble adjusting to a new culture . . .'

'Alex has been here since he was a boy!' Miranda began to cry. She told the teacher how tired she was of being the odd person in the family, that we passed secret signals behind her back. My teacher handed her tissues and moved closer to her on the chair.

I watched them. I could hardly believe that this was my mother. I was nothing like her; she was nothing like my family. This woman was for 'Alex,' as she called my father, whining and crying and baby-talking.

'Alex lets him drink, too. Only ten years old and he can have vodka whenever he asks. His *grandmother* gives it to him. I can't make them stop. They all just look at me like I'm intruding on their business.'

'Dear me, that is serious. I think he's far too young to be drinking hard liquor.'

'Don't you have a doctor that can talk to him?'

'Maybe we can arrange something, Mrs Dal. He does seem to have problems relating to some of the other children. He's a loner, but I do see him playing well now and then.'

I couldn't hold still any longer. 'That's because they don't like *me*.'

Both of them looked at me as if they'd forgotten I was there.

I closed the book on my desk. I was going to leave. Papa said not to talk about things to outsiders. But I was angry and they were stupid.

'Why do you think they don't like you?' my teacher asked.

'I *know* they don't like me.' It was a powerful thing to admit that. I felt suddenly that I had the freedom to say what was certain. 'They don't even want to touch me. They think that we are Communists.'

'Did they tell you that?'

'No, but when anyone talks about Communists, they look at me. They're wondering about it. Maybe they think I'll drop an atom bomb on them.'

'How do you know? They don't say these things, do they?'

'I know,' I said. I had to show them how much more I knew than they did, the stupid women. 'I know because I have the power to know. I have . . . ' I started to say it, but I didn't. Papa had warned me never to talk about the *pozhar-golava*, not even to my mother.

'Yes, but – '

'I know what you feel,' I said to my teacher, who was frowning at me as if I were misbehaving. 'I know that Lynne is your favorite, every time she raises her hand you're proud. You've never even noticed me except when I forget and speak my language. You think I'm slow, don't you, because you feel impatient with me. And you hate

42

Barney because he writes backhand and comes to school dirty. And Linda is afraid of you, because you stand over her when she does arithmetic and it makes her so nervous she can't think. I know that you're happy whenever Mr McCollough . . . '

'That's enough!' my teacher said. She stood up. 'You don't know what you're talking about.'

My mother pointed at me. 'See what a hateful boy he is?'

I don't know why I did it. Probably because I had just told them the greatest and most powerful thing that existed for me, and they just scorned it. I was surprised, then angry, and the first thought was to strike. I still had my book in my hands. I picked it up and threw it at both of them – it didn't matter which one or whether it hit. It caught my mother on the shoulder, which I glimpsed as I began to run.

I was down the hallway before they could get out of the classroom. Over the chainlink fence, down into the dry irrigation ditch, sheltered by cotton-woods. I moved with the energy of terror. I ran for blocks and blocks, stopping only once to look behind me. No one followed.

Don't know how many hours I walked, then sat, but when it was dark, I found myself at old Mr Litvak's liquor store. He was always kind to me when we went in there, sometimes giving me candy if he had it; sometimes a penny. I went in the door and looked at Mr Litvak behind the counter, not knowing what to say or do.

'What's this?' he asked me in Russian. 'Where's your papa?'

'Please, Mr Litvak, may I have something to drink?'

'I can give you a *soda*,' he said, using the English word, 'if you have a nickel.'

I reached into my pockets. 'But I would like some vodka.'

I had no money. Mr Litvak laughed and told me he couldn't give me vodka. I told him that I couldn't go home, that I was going to go to New York City tonight, but was thirsty.

'Why do you want to go to New York City?'

'Grandfather says they have a big library there.'

'Oh, so you like to read, do you, Kolya?'

'Yes, sir.'

'I have some books at home that you might like to read.'

I was interested. Mr Litvak was feeling kindly toward me. He called his wife. I had a free soda, and waited on the stool by the cash register with him until Mrs Litvak came in her big car. They talked to each other in a language I didn't understand. It was probably Yiddish. Mrs Litvak took me home with her.

She fed me dinner – stewed chicken, I think – and red jello. She was nice to me, but nervous about having me there. The Litvaks had no children. She didn't know what to do with me. She told me that some of her family had known some of my family a long time ago, and then she offered me a little glass of wine. I sipped it; it was too sweet, but I drank it. Then she showed me the books that Mr Litvak had mentioned.

There were many books in Russian and English. Most of the Russian books were too dull for a boy my age, but I looked through all the pictures. It was the first time I saw the word pogrom, which sounded like a good word at first. I liked the way it sounded, but there were pictures of weeping people being driven away by Cossacks and that was a little frightening.

'Here's a book with pictures,' Mrs Litvak said, pulling down a big art book. I looked at it for a long time. What I can remember now is that it was a volume of art master-pieces. There were Greek statues, vases, Renaissance Christian art, Edward Hopper's painting of the diner, and also carvings. I looked for a long time at the Chinese jade.

My father came. I was glad to see him. I was sleepy. Soon Mr Litvak came home, too. Papa seemed anxious to leave and the Litvaks were also uncomfortable, so I didn't resist when Papa said he wanted to take me home.

When we got into the car, he asked me for my side of the story. I told him. I apologized for having said the things I wasn't supposed to, but my anger with Miranda ('Mother,' Papa corrected, and 'Mother' I repeated) was still there.

Papa didn't say much. He put his hand on my head and left it there for a long time as he drove.

My mother was gone when I got home. I never asked about her again until much later, when my father and I became friends once more.

I was paralyzed by the knock on my apartment door. I stood only inches from it. Do I let him in and act as if there is nothing to be afraid of? Then he would go for ever, and it would be over.

But I wasn't ready. A second knock rattled the door.

The person on the other side was so close to me, separated only by the wooden slab of a door. It began to rain harder. I touched the doorknob, but I knew my hand wouldn't turn it. I listened to him.

The man on the other side was a good man. I know that somehow. That is a simple statement for a complex person, however. But he is looking for something. He wants to accomplish something. Not a villain, not to himself, anyway. I'm sure he has the best intentions in the world, but no, no, thank you, you don't understand.

We stood, each waiting. And then he decided to leave.

Leaving. I felt his disappointment.

I know he will be back another time. I could feel that about him. I will be more prepared next time. I was shaking so badly that I could hardly have acted anything but guilty.

I went to the bathroom and looked out the window. The man under the umbrella paused at the side of the house. Someone else was coming back the other way. It was Jack. They passed each other quickly without saying anything, as far as I could see.

I heard her come up the steps. I looked out the kitchen window and saw the umbrella man go to his car.

Should I let Jack in, I wondered?

I never saw the man's face because I ran to my door to open it for her. I needed to have her to calm me down,

45

distract me. I grabbed her and hugged her; she was all wet because she'd come through the rain without an umbrella.

'Did you see that man?' I asked her, trying to sound natural.

'A man?'

'In the yard.'

'Oh, yeah. Why?'

'I hope he didn't see you come up here. He's an insurance agent and I'm avoiding him.'

'Oh.' She pulled away from me and began to take her jacket off. 'I hope you don't mind me just dropping by. Since you don't have a phone.'

'No, I'm glad to see you.' I kissed the top of her head. 'You didn't speak to me the other day and I thought you were going to ignore me for the rest of the semester.'

'When was that?' she said, surprised.

'In class.'

'Oh, no, I didn't see you. Sorry.' She flopped down. 'How are you? You look . . . Have I interrupted anything?'

I sat down beside her and spread the newspaper at our feet. My hands were still trembling. 'I was looking for a new place to live.'

'Moving? But why?'

'I've just decided that I want to.'

She crossed her arms around her knees and rested her chin, folded up into a tidy package. With a wistful sigh, she said, 'Wish I could move.'

I could feel it begin. I needed to get into the kitchen to have a drink. I didn't know how to do it because she was so watchful. She was really and seriously depressed. It was starting to roll out of her toward me. I found refuge in some physical distance by moving to the window. I lit a cigarette.

The umbrella man's car had gone now.

The distance wasn't far enough. I started to feel prickly; her demons were pursuing me. I headed toward the kitchen. 'Coffee?'

'Sure,' she said.

I went to the kitchen, opened the cupboard, took a drink,

46

and started the coffee. I didn't want to leave the kitchen, so I puttered around, hanging a potholder on a hook, washing out the pan from last night's dinner, wiping the cupboard. Jack came and stood at the door.

'Are you sure it's all right that I came over?'

'I guess I'm still a bit sleepy,' I said. 'I'll be livelier company in a little while. After more coffee.'

She was uncertain about me. She started to move away from the door. I guessed that she might leave, unless I did something. She was ill at ease. I couldn't decide if I wanted her or not. The lust had cooled. It seemed as if that night we'd made love so magnificently had already happened far in the past, sometime when we had both been younger.

A result of the umbrella man's visit was a sensation of being watched, which clouded everything I did. I wanted to get on the bus to Denver and run to my father, but the most practical consideration was to get moved. Today. And Jack has a truck.

Besides all that, in the few seconds of Jack moving away from the kitchen doorway, I saw something in my mind – I saw Jack giving me an acquaintance's nod in the hallways at school, maybe stopping at the desk in the library to say hello and ask after my health.

I didn't want that. I didn't want an enormous distance between us. I was just getting to know her and I liked what I knew.

'Susanna Pavlovna,' I said, coming out of the kitchen.

'Don't call me that,' she said, smiling. A little sound came from her throat as I squeezed her up in a hug.

We undressed each other. We were covered with sprinklings of rain shadows from the windows. Jack stroked my chest (I always wished I was descended from Italians with their dark skin and furry chests, but Jack didn't seem to think of this at all). 'I was thinking of you last night,' she said. 'I could hardly wait to see you again.'

'You shouldn't have.'

'Have you been drinking already?' she asked after a kiss.

'Yes, but don't think about that.' I spoke with my face in

47

her hair. She squirmed a little under me, as if she wanted to move, but I didn't let her. 'I have to drink, don't worry about it.' I looked at her face.

She was a little frightened by me, but she no longer tried to get away. 'Are you an alcoholic?' she asked.

'No. I drink. Do you really want to talk about this right now?' I smiled at her. Slowly, the worry passed out of her face and she smiled back at me.

I was dosed up, and didn't feel it the same way I had nights ago, but Jack was even more passionate than before. I wished . . . I wished I hadn't had anything to drink before we made love.

But. She's high voltage. Danger. It is better that I protect myself.

We lay silently for a time afterwards. Jack closed her eyes. She seemed to doze and wake, doze and wake. I just held her and thought about many things.

'Kolya,' she said quietly, sleepily.

'Yes?'

'May I go with you to look for apartments?'

'Of course.' Life can be simple. I wanted a cigarette, but I didn't want to move away from her. I was happy for the moment, in my way.

'Why *do* you drink?' she asked.

'I have a genetic defect. It gives me a pain in the head and alcohol is medicine.'

'What kind of defect?'

'It's very complicated.'

'But what's it called?'

'I don't remember.'

'How do you know you have it?'

'My family is full of idiots who have to drink to cure the pain in their heads.'

She laughed. 'You're joking with me.'

'No, I'm not. I'm serious. I've even had a vasectomy to stop the genes from getting passed on. I'm the last of them.'

Her expression changed, darkened, and her gaze left me. She rolled onto her back and stared up toward the ceiling.

'The last one,' she said, slowly. 'My father's the last male Berdo. I wonder why that's important.'

I was thinking about my father. I had never been able to tell him about the vasectomy. Some day I would have to. It seemed easier to tell anyone else in the world what I'd done to strangle the Dal line than him. He somehow never seemed to see the problem of it all. He is so even, so loving. I think he likes to wallow in other people's morasses, though when it comes to his own he has no idea what to do.

I was sweating.

She was thinking about her mother, I could see that. I touched her face with my fingertips. 'Susanne,' I said.

'Don't call me that.'

'Why?'

'That's my mother's name.'

'Don't you like your mother?'

'Yes, I love her. Of course, I like her.' She sounded irritated. She sat up. I admired the way she moved.

'It's a beautiful name.'

Jack sighed. She reached for her underwear. 'May I borrow your shower?' She stood, the blue panties dangling from her fingers.

'I don't want you to go yet,' I said, on my knees, pressing my face against her belly. She was softer than most girls. She was lovely, and smelled like sex. I wanted her again.

'We'd better get going. You don't want to miss the apartment of your dreams, do you?'

I let her go, stretched and poured some coffee. I sat and looked at the newspaper again while she showered. I looked out the window – the umbrella man's car was not back. No, he wouldn't come back today, somehow I knew that. I was safe a little longer. I can pick up my mail here for a while, then put in a change of address at the post office later.

I smoked two cigarettes while Jack was in the bathroom. The room filled with striated layers of blue smoke. I waved my hand and finally opened the window a little. It was cool outside. I looked around the room to collect my jacket, find clean underwear. Jack came out and stood in the hallway.

'What's the matter?' I asked.

She walked forward slowly. 'If you had a wife for twenty-some years, and she was dying, how do you think you would act?'

I shook my head. An impossible question. First of all, I would have to stay drunk. Secondly, I would probably expire of that knowledge. But, if I were someone else . . . 'I don't know.'

'My father,' she said softly, 'has turned into a bad night-club act. You know – in a dismal resort where no one is having a good time, and he tells jokes to cheer up a sour audience? I hate him.'

'What was he like before?'

'Ordinary.'

'Everyone thinks their parents either too ordinary or too bizarre. Was he a comedian before?'

Jack shook her head. She dressed. 'He told us not to talk to her.'

'Us?' I asked.

'My little sister, Julie, and me.'

'Do you want to talk to your mother?'

'I don't know what to say.'

'Then wait until you think of something.'

She sat down on the straight-backed chair at the desk. 'I don't know what to say,' she repeated, and hung her head.

I drank my coffee and looked out the window. Jack was silent, but not weeping.

'I wish there was just one thing I could do for her. One thing that would really mean something to her . . . before.'

I couldn't stand it. I went into the kitchen and took another little drink. I leaned into the sink and watched the rusty water dripping onto the old flat porcelain. Strange how you notice things when you're feeling upset – I had never looked at that sink so carefully before. I thought about the plumbing of the entire house as I stood there. And felt as empty as the drain.

'I didn't mean to depress you,' Jack said.

I turned. 'It's not me you need to worry about, is it?'

'No.'

I took my shower, dressed, and carried the newspaper out the door, following Jack. She was anxious to go. I couldn't help but stop at the landing and survey the neighborhood for that blue car the umbrella man had been in. Jack had parked out in front this time – why? How did she find the place? But this is her home town. I never used the front to exit or enter. I looked up and down the block as we crossed the lawn to her truck.

In the truck, I started to pull a cigarette from my pocket, thought better of it, and put my hands back in my pockets. I told her the first address. We drove in silence for a few blocks. I didn't like the silence, but couldn't think of much to say to her. I finally thought of something to ask her about.

'How does an anthropology major get so worked up over Richard the Third?' I said.

She blushed. 'I can't believe I said those things in front of the whole class that day.'

'But why?'

'Oh, novels, I guess. I read a few that had Richard in them, always a baby-eating villain, then I read one in which he was treated a little more realistically – not necessarily the best person in the world, but at least slightly human. Then I looked up stuff in history books. I decided it was a matter of faith – just the way you want to believe, although the reasons are stacked up for the Tudors. There's no way really to know. It's like being raised a Protestant or Hindu, Democrat or Communist . . . It doesn't matter how much you know about things, it's how you interpret them. My guts want to believe that Richard was not so awful, and I have facts that can back it up to a certain point.'

'But not all the way.'

'No. That's where faith comes in. What kind of man would kill his nephews? The Tudors were really awful people when you look at the facts.'

'I suppose so. But then you can forgive them their crimes, too, if you like. Things were different then. Public

51

scandal didn't hurt people like it does now. They just said "fuck 'em" and went on about their business. My God, what Henry did with his wives! If anyone deserves a little forgiveness I suppose it should be a wife. But, just because he was not the same family doesn't make Richard much better than the Tudors, does it?'

She just smiled. 'He didn't do it, I'm sure. Whether he could have done it doesn't matter, because I don't think he did. I'll lend you the books sometime.'

'Novels?'

'Don't you read novels?'

'As often as I can.'

'Oh, good. I meet so many people who think fiction is a waste of time.'

We were quiet again, but it had a different, companionable quality this time. Jack took a slow route through the campus. Cars stopped in the narrow streets by the dormitories, letting people out, collecting them.

'Are you going to take classes this summer, too?' she asked.

'Probably. I haven't seen the schedule yet. I usually go back and forth to my grandmother's a lot then, but I can finish by December if I work hard this summer.'

'Guess I'll get a job this summer. Shit! Have to be a waitress or something like that. Last year I worked as a typist and was bored out of my mind. No flexibility in schedule, either. Maybe I can find something more interesting this year. Maybe I should change my major, do something useful like data processing, or nursing . . . '

'Yeech,' I said.

She laughed. 'I don't know how you live on the work-study money. I looked into that and it's not much to live on if you're on your own.'

'My father lives cheap. He sends me money. And my grandmother has a bit to give away.'

'I didn't mean . . . '

'That's all right. Money doesn't embarrass me, I'm neither rich nor poor enough for that kind of embarrassment.' I pointed to an old house, not unlike the one I live in already. 'I think this is the place.' But there were six mailboxes attached to the front porch. Too many people in such a small area. We got out of the truck. As Jack inspected the porch and the yard, I rang the bell marked as the manager's.

'The apartment's rented,' a man said, opening the door.

'Thank you.' I was relieved.

Jack seemed a little sad as we returned to the truck. 'I guess he wouldn't have been a good landlord anyway. Too curt.'

'Was he?'

We drove to the next, though I realized it was further from the school than I liked. It was a garage apartment, one wide and spacious room, lots of windows. I liked it, especially as the building stood apart and I would be the only human occupant. But a dog yapped in the yard and children ran down the alley. Jack mentioned that there were no closets, the kitchen sink was tiny, the refrigerator old, and other things that I didn't care about. I felt a little reserved about it because of her, though it seemed like a good place.

'What do I need closets for?' I asked.

Jack just shrugged. 'Well, it's not up to me.'

I told the woman showing it that I wanted to see another place or two and would let her know this afternoon.

'Better not wait too long,' she said.

I knew she was right; it was likely to be gone in another hour. But there was something wrong with it, or maybe it was just Jack's head-shaking that had gotten to me. I decided to take it if the next place wasn't agreeable. I read her the next address when we got into the truck. It meant nothing to me.

'That's on the same side of town as my house.'

'Oh. Too far from campus, then, isn't it?'

'Well, it's far, but near a bus line, and not so far and hilly that you couldn't ride your bike.'

'All right.' I didn't want to live near Jack, that was

certain. I started thinking that we should go back to the last place and I would take it.

She turned a corner near the location. A small row of businesses – a hardware store, liquor store, small grocer and a second-hand shop – gave it an old neighborhood look. 'That would be convenient,' I said.

'I know which store you're looking at.'

Virtuous bitch. I sulked, but lightly, because she only meant to tease me.

She pulled over to the curb in front of a duplex. We found the owner, who lived in the other side and he opened up. This one did have closets. Two. One for coats and boots, another in the bedroom. And a bedroom, for God's sake. Bedrooms are luxuries for people who have graduated. The kitchen was small, a little shabby, but enameled mint-green right down to the small wooden table and three wooden chairs.

I felt safe in this house. I stood there and felt it. It was all right. The couple who owned it lived on the other side of the carport. He seemed like a mild old man, though he acted a bit gruff.

'I'll knock your rent down if you do our yardwork,' he said.

I looked out of the window. Trees, a rather dry and scrubby lawn, a decent view of the mountains out of the front door and windows. The lawn had a slope, but what the hell, I can use the exercise. I agreed to it all, but didn't have the money for the deposit, first and last month's rent.

Jack came beside me and said softly, 'Don't worry about that.'

I looked at her. One would think that she was moving, too, the way she'd gone around looking in the closets, lifting the back off the toilet, checking under the sink. She was having a wonderful time.

But she was too close. I felt her hands on my life suddenly, and wished that I hadn't brought her along.

'May I pay you the deposit and first month's rent, then double rent next month?' I asked.

The landlord scratched his skinny arm, turning toward the door, a deliberately skeptical move. 'Well, I tell you, renting out to students isn't always the best business and I would really rather . . . '

'Don't worry about it,' Jack said, louder this time. She touched my sleeve. 'You can pay me back.'

I felt harassed. I really did like this place. It was quiet, isolated, roomy. 'All right.' I took out my check book, and Jack took out hers. We handed our checks over and he gave me a key.

'I'll bring a lease over when I see you come back,' he said, and left us alone in the house.

Jack, still sitting cross-legged on the floor where she'd written her check, looked up at me. 'Have I made you angry?'

'No.' I went into the kitchen and looked at the enameled chairs. But somehow I was terribly depressed. I turned the tap on and watched the water run – it was less rusty than in my apartment. This place was too large. I started having regrets. If I'd taken the last place, perhaps I would have been happier. I sat down in one of the chairs. My hands felt weird; I worked them. I was sad, filled with dread and didn't want to move from my chair . . .

Jack.

'Jack! We have to get going!' I shouted. I jumped up and walked into the living room. There she sat, her hands clenched together in her lap. She looked at me sadly. I was already getting into a sweat. 'Come on,' I said, trying to bully her out of her mood. 'I'll buy you a hamburger if you help me move my books.'

She rose.

'Look, isn't this a great place?' I said, pointing around the house. 'So much room. Those are great windows, too.' And they are, old sash-weighted windows with six panes in each frame. I could imagine warm summer mornings pouring in through them.

Our mood improved. By the time we got into the truck, Jack was smiling again.

'It'll be a terrific place,' I said, hoping I didn't sound too frantic. 'Thank you for helping me out.'

'You're welcome.'

She still wasn't out of her depression, though she was better. I had to try harder to distract, entertain or irritate her. I was getting hot, so hot I could have taken my shirt off in the car to be more comfortable. Sweat rolled down my sides, down from my scalp around my ears. How stupid of me to choose this woman for a companion, even for a few hours at a time. I wiped my face with my sleeve.

'May I smoke a cigarette?' I asked.

'Not in my truck, please,' she said. 'I can't stand the smoke in such a small place.'

'I'm sorry.'

We drove on. I couldn't think of anything to say. I didn't know how to divert her. She was relentlessly somber. Feeling desperate, I said, 'Jack, stop a minute. Pull over.'

She parked and looked at me, worried.

I clutched my leg. 'Having a cramp. Let me walk a minute. You stay here.' I got out and walked up and down the sidewalk for a minute or so, feigning a limp. My head began to clear, I began to cool off. Jack got out and stood by the hood.

'You don't get enough calcium in your diet,' she said. 'Or exercise.'

'Is that it?' I moved toward the truck, evaluating whether I could get back into such close range of her, but she seemed less introspective at the moment. 'We should stop and get some boxes, you know.'

'Good idea.'

We drove to a small shopping center and found a mountain of boxes behind a liquor store. We threw them into the back of the truck. Playfully, I hit Jack on the head with a box. She giggled. What a relief.

We carried the boxes up my stairs. They made a hollow clonking sound as they bounced together. As Jack started loading them with books, I slipped into the kitchen and sucked at my bottle.

When the moving actually began, every minute in the apartment made me nervous. I wondered if the umbrella man had come back; I wondered if he were watching me from somewhere nearby. I left Jack packing (which she seemed to enjoy, looking over all my books and things without reserve) and went downstairs to talk to my land-lady.

'What? Moving?' Her old red face got redder and she shuffled back into the safety of her kitchen. She wore a faded dress and shabby terry cloth slippers. A suspicious look came into her face. I realized that she was making a connection between this and the umbrella man.

'Are you in trouble or something?' she asked.

'Trouble? No, not at all. I've . . . well, to tell you the truth, I've found a lovely roommate and the apartment is too small for both of us.'

'Why don't kids get married any more?' she complained. 'I would rather you lived somewhere else, anyway, if that's what's going on.'

Then I was embarrassed. I had never the slightest idea that she thought about anything other than the amount of butter and flour she possessed.

'Who was that man – police?'

'What man?' I asked, and suddenly my pulse was hard.

'This morning.'

'I don't know.'

'Just before the girl came.'

Oh, so she did notice that, too. I was relieved because it added to the credibility of my excuse for a sudden move. 'I was in the bath. What did he say?'

'He asked me if you live here.'

'Did he give a name?'

'No.'

'What did he look like?'

'Dark man. Sounded like a easterner or something.' She looked at me closely, hoping I would recognize him from her astute description. 'Well-dressed. Maybe a lawyer?'

I shrugged. 'I don't know.'

'Well, it sounded important. Where are you going to be?'

'I'll come by and get my mail. I can't remember the address right now.' I realized that I wasn't going to be able to put in a change of address for a time. 'I think that man was just selling insurance or something. I don't want to talk to a salesman. Just tell him I've moved back to Denver if he comes back.'

'Is that where you're going?'

'No.'

'Why can't you tell the truth then?' She looked suspicious again. 'He *was* a lawyer, wasn't he?'

'I don't know,' I said impatiently.

'You clean up that apartment real well, okay?'

'Yes, ma'am.' I mocked her homely accent, but she didn't notice.

I hurried outside and had a sudden panicky thought that the umbrella man might have returned and Jack would just be sitting up there chatting away with him. But as I came to the stairway, she appeared at the doorway, carrying a box. I backed down and waited for her at the bottom.

'Lucky I met a woman with a truck,' I said.

'Well, I expect something in return.'

'Yes.'

'More than that. I've been thinking – for the price of the damage deposit, may I have a key?'

'What?' I couldn't believe what she was asking. She wasn't kidding either. For eight years, I've lived alone with all the privacy that I need (not want, but *need*) and here was this person of only a few weeks' acquaintance asking me for a key. 'No, I don't think so,' I said.

'No, I don't mean . . . ' She made a desperate face. 'I don't want to intrude, but if I could just have a place to go to, maybe during the day when you're at class or at work. I don't want to *live* with you. I wouldn't be there much. Just a place for me to go when things get rough at home. I'll knock first. You can tell me to go away if you're there. Really.'

I carried the box of books to the truck. The truck bed

58

was wet from the rain. 'My books are going to get damp.'

'Kolya, listen. I wouldn't bother you. Really,' she said. 'I know how it sounds, but I'll be like a silent roommate. No, I won't even be like a roommate. I'll help you with the rent, if you like, but I'll only go there when you're not there, or if it's okay with you. I promise.'

I looked at her. It was clearly impossible. I could hear a strangely familiar cry from her for a sanctuary, but *my* life was no sanctuary for anyone, not even me. I thought of my things, letters, photographs, things that might – well, there isn't much physical evidence of anything. Especially if one doesn't understand the language. But . . .

'If you knew how things are at home,' she said quietly, 'you would understand that I need a place to go to. I'm not trying to move in on you, I just see . . . Well, I guess it looks that way, doesn't it?'

'I understand,' I said. I did. It was my curse to understand. And I thought of the money – any money helps.

'You can have other women over, you can smoke, drink and go on with your life.' She was beginning to feel that she'd pushed me too far. Physically, she backed away from me, her eyes averted. 'Oh, well, I'm sorry. It's a pretty stupid idea, I guess. I'm being pushy again. I get like that.'

I had a sudden eerie sense of recognition, as if someone had just read my tarot cards, or done my palm and told me something was about to happen to me.

This woman is going to change my life, I thought. Somehow. But it wasn't anything as simple as fall in love, get married, things like that. Something was going to change and I knew it. Just looking at her face, I felt it happening already.

Like a thaw.

'All right,' I said. 'But let's just try it out and talk about it in a couple of weeks. Okay?'

'Oh, Kolya, thank you. You don't know.'

Oh, yes I do, yes I do.

We worked hard. Jack was incredibly cheerful, whistling, laughing at me and what I possess with a good-natured sense of discovery. I didn't feel that she was critical of me at all; in fact, she *likes* me. She made me feel good.

Before the last few loads, I called Gus and Freda. The four of us went for hamburgers and beer. Gus and Freda seem to be getting along, which made me happy. They helped us move the last of the boxes, then left Jack and me alone in the new place.

Jack lay on the floor with her bare feet up against the wall. Her hair rippled out around her head, black, silver-shot, against the dull avocado-colored carpet. Words and sounds echoed around the house. My bookcases barely fill a corner of the living room, the desk and chair another. The mattresses have been exiled to the bedroom, where my clothes hang in the closet. Food and dishes are shelved in the kitchen. The starkness pleases me. I can see everything. Painted in pale colors, the rooms are bright. Empty.

I poured myself a drink and stepped over Jack to settle on the floor beside her.

'I don't understand how you can drink that straight down,' she said.

Feeling so happy that everything had gone well, that I'd escaped the umbrella man and was sitting at home with a pleasant and attractive friend, I laughed.

'Don't you want a telephone?' she asked.

'Can't afford it. Besides, I don't make that many calls.'

'Oh.' She looked around to the corner where the book-case stands. 'You know, we could go to the second-hand store tomorrow to try to find a lamp. You need another lamp.'

'Don't have any money left now. And tomorrow I'm going to Denver. Visiting day for little Nicholas at Grand-mama's.'

'Oh.' She watched me. 'Have you ever lived with a woman?'

'No.' I toasted her with a vodka glass, but didn't dare say she was the first, because she isn't going to get that far. 'I am transparently unreformable, I guess, and no one wants to live with that.'

She started to ask something else, but didn't. I knew what it was so I answered for her.

'I've never wanted to anyway.'

She turned her face away. There are many reasons, but it was never entirely my fault that there are few women who care about a perpetual student, without money, who is overly attached to a family that speaks another language even in company, and who drinks too much. Besides, I don't have charm and good looks, but this pinched and intense face with dull grey eyes and then a bad posture, too. Not the American dream.

'I've been in love a few times,' she said, 'but when I look back, it was all sort of silly and made-up. I always just thought it was time for me to be in love. I have too much to do now anyway – grad school and Europe.'

'Well, I'm safe enough for you then,' I said.

A sharp look. 'Why do you say that?'

'I won't be the one, either.'

She sat up. 'Kolya, you're wonderful,' she said, surprised. 'You don't think much of yourself, do you? You're fascinating. You're different, I like that.'

'Thank you,' I said, uncomfortably. I didn't want to hear her rationalization of why she was sleeping and spending time with me.

'I have decided,' she said, leaning toward me, 'to be as honest as I can with people. I'm going to let them know what I'm thinking and feeling. I don't want to get into the position that my mother's in, where she lives with a family that can't even open its mouth for an honest conversation.'

'Yes, well, I know what you feel most of the time,' I said, smiling (she has no idea!), 'because you are rather open anyway.'

'Except at home.'

I didn't want to hear about home. In fact, I was getting edgy and hoping that Jack would go there now.

'I still can't talk to her.'

'Who?'

'My mother. I know that there's not much time.'

'Just talk to her.'

'I can't. We're all watching each other. We clump together, and Dad never lets us be alone with her because he's afraid we'll upset her. He doesn't want us to mention anything about it.'

I said 'mm-hm' and got up to pour a little more vodka.

'You don't want to talk about it, either.'

I didn't say anything. I came back into the living room but just stood there, surveying the new surroundings. I was just a little drunk. Didn't want to drink any more, but Jack was going to get upset about her mother again. I really wanted just to sit alone, at my desk here, and just . . . *maunder*. It was unfortunate timing for me to have had my fill of her company, but it happened that way.

There was a real silence. Jack stood. 'Guess I'll go now.'

'Jack,' I said, 'sometime we'll talk about it, but not now.'

'Not now,' she repeated, as if they were familiar words to be mocked. She went to the door. 'Good night.' And she was gone.

I didn't move for a long time afterwards.

Kolya, you're an ass.

11 March

After supper, Grandmama and I sat on the patio chairs on the dark porch. The weather had been nice all day. I had dozed a little on the bus, with the sun shining in my face, and think I have a bit of sunburn. Felt queasy this morning – mixing Gus's beer with my vodka, but Grandmama's food fixed that.

At first, she wanted to talk of nothing but the man who'd come to visit, but I told her that it was nothing to worry about. I didn't tell her about him coming to my apartment – who knows, isn't it possible he's not the same man at all?

It was a warm spring night. The couple across the street were entertaining another couple. Their combined force of children all seemed to be in the 'looky-looky' stage, and every now and then a reprimand and a wail would sound out as little fingers got into flower pots and books. A man down the street worked on his motorcycle in the garage. He tinkered, then mounted the bike. It roared tremendously, then he hopped off and tinkered again.

I don't know many of these people on this block any more, though I've grown up here. Long ago, it was an old neighborhood, filled with old couples who had bought their houses new. They started to die, retire to senior citizen condominiums and such; others came to rent, buy, and the world changed. People don't stay in the same houses all their lives any more.

I thought of what Grandfather had said about home in the old country: 'People lived in the same house – father to son, father to son. Sometimes, when there were too many sons, they would build a new house nearby, taking a birch from the old property.'

'What do you think he would want with us anyway?'

I shrugged. I had an idea. But I was thinking instead about living again in that house some day. There would be no one to give the house to when I died. Perhaps I will give everything to a medical center, including an explanation of the Dal family. This journal, perhaps? That should interest the head-hunters, besides telling them a thing or two.

'I worry, Kolya,' Grandmother said. 'I've seen that people in this country like to make money from things that are strange. Someone will make a movie on you, and they'll make it so people won't leave you alone.'

'They don't leave us alone, anyway.' But, now that I think about it, it is easy to hide and be anonymous in America.

'What would life be like if . . .'

I took her hand. 'Don't think about it. Don't. Old Nicholas Pavlovich shouldn't have had sons.'

I wonder sometimes, when she says these things, if she has been thinking them all these years of living in America, and just began to say them to me as I grew up. Or did she start her regrets when she became a widow? Sometimes, it seemed that she had not thought about anything on her own until Grandfather died.

'Oh, we didn't care back then, Kolya. I knew everything when I married Fyodor – even my father didn't mind. The Dals could make a good life for me. And I'm not sorry I had my Sasha. I wanted my babies.' Tears began. 'I'm not sorry, but I wish your father would come to see me.'

I lit a cigarette. I felt a lot of pain of my own, and hers.

When I got home tonight, I realized there is a flaw in my new home. I hate coming and going on the street. I miss the alley entrance. Now I have to unlock my door with the whole world watching.

I felt something strange as soon as I entered. Was someone sitting in the room, or standing in the kitchen, or lying on my bed? I couldn't sense a person, but I sensed *something*.

'Jack?' No answer.

I turned on the light. A rocking chair and standing lamp had been added to the furnishings, by the bookcases. So Jack has been here in my absence. I closed the door and went into the bedroom. She had also bought a chest of drawers, a little rickety, but nothing I couldn't cure with a few nails, maybe some glue. Jack had scoffed at my box of underwear in the bottom of the closet. The closet. I checked my letter box and saw that the tape on the ends was undisturbed.

I opened the first drawer of the chest. Empty. The second stuck. Only the bottom drawer contained anything: two panties, a T-shirt, a pair of knee socks, a scratch pad and pen (in case she gets locked in the bedroom, to send paper airplane messages for help?). I picked up the paper. After all, this is my house, I may inspect what it contains. I know that I wouldn't stand for the reverse, but I wouldn't leave my things somewhere obvious if they were private.

A tiny corner of white cardboard stuck out from under the T-shirt. I pulled it out.

It was a photograph of a younger Jack with longer hair and a cocky grin, sitting with a woman. Both of them smiled sideways at the photographer, who had apparently just caught their attention.

This hadn't been my expectation of the elder Susanne. I'd imagined the poor tragic dowdy housewife who submitted to and nagged her family dutifully. No. This woman was far from that. She looked small and fragile already then, that many (three, four?) years ago. She had incredible silver hair, a dark streak only at the crown. Shyness subdued the smile, but not those eyes.

I looked at the photo for a long time. I don't know why, I don't know what I was looking for, but I studied that face.

And now she is dying. She was already so frail and she was . . . she was so beautiful that I ached. It was the hair – the light in the photograph seemed to be bright sun from a window beside them – and her eyes, dark like Jack's, haunted me.

Would I give Susanne Berdo a second glance if I didn't know she was dying?

Yes, I think I would. Even from a small Kodacolor print, she has extraordinary presence. I have, over the years, been able to match faces with the internal workings of people. Ah, they say, don't judge by appearance, but it isn't the regularity of features, the resemblance to celebrities that I see. It's a person inside expressing through the boldness/timidity of their eyes, the composure of their mouth, that attitude of the chin. I do not see beauty in the way others might, but even the harshest judge would say Susanne was attractive. I wonder what she looks like now.

I finally tucked the photo under the clothes and shut the drawer. In the kitchen, I found a note from Jack:

Kolya,
    The rocking chair was only ten dollars, the chest only five-fifty at a garage sale. What a deal, huh? I put some cookies in the cookie jar for you.
                                   Jack

Cookie jar? I looked on the counter top and there was a big ceramic bunny with a fat belly, sitting on its shiny haunches. Cute. I opened it and found homemade chocolate chip cookies. Am eating them now and soon I'll go to bed.

12 March

I've had strange dreams.

I fell asleep in the rocking chair with my chemistry text on my lap, thinking about the relationship between sodium and lithium.

I dreamt about the Flame. The candle flame had a face, and it was Susanne's face, all oily and shiny, her silver hair was blue flame. I was surprised to see her like that, and she said, 'Didn't you know? I've always been here. You just didn't know what you were looking at.'

She took a little square of white wax in her hands, larger than a bar of soap, huge in her tiny fingers, because she was only as big as a candle.

'I don't know what that is,' I said.

'Of course you do. Watch.' She peeled it as if her fingers had become knives, pieces of wax curling away then melting. As they dropped away, they burst into flames and disappeared.

She handed me the carving. It looked like a fetus, but was heavy and slug-like. I recoiled from it. 'I don't want it.'

'I do, and I'm not sorry I had my babies.' Her face was old, like Grandmama's.

Jack knocked at my door.

It was only dawn. I was kinked up from sitting in the chair. I let her in. She looked awful; I sensed danger.

'My mother's puking her guts out. I had to leave,' she said. 'I'm sorry I woke you up.'

'Maybe this isn't going to work,' I said, sleepy, irritated, and now I had to get a drink on an empty stomach at this time of day.

'Kolya, I'm sorry. I'll never do it again.' She sat down in the chair I'd spent the night in. 'Next time I'll just come in without waking you up.'

I hurried to the kitchen and took a little drink – just enough to quiet my brain. It didn't sit right, but I needed it.

'Come on,' I said, and took her by the hand. We went into the bedroom, undressed, and snuggled down. It was nice to be in bed after sitting all night, and I enjoyed having her naked against me. I started to feel her with my hands and she started touching me in return. It didn't take long before we were at it, at first just friendly and natural, then something in her started tugging at me deeply. It got a little more frantic, then, Christ, I was shattered and raw at the end of it, but very satisfied. It was so good it woke me up completely, because I wanted to think about it, but Jack fell asleep.

I tried to see her face in the dark. She stretched and sighed in her sleep (or half-sleep), and I could only see the oval shape of her face in the dark, the hair spattered over her shoulders. She was still, her breath so shallow that it barely seemed enough to sustain her. I put my fingers over her mouth and checked the warm air passing out from her nose and lips. She smelled good. I kissed her as she slept.

We went off to school together this morning. I didn't have anything to do for two hours, so had coffee in the student union, then looked at the bulletin boards, wandered through the bookstore and bought a paperback about socialists in the 1930s, then sat outside. A few blades of grass have turned green; the sky was absolutely cloudless and blue. It is never that blue in Denver any more, because of the pollution, though it had been when I was young. The season is groaning to change, and the air smells sweet – a damp, growing green and woody smell.

It was all so new, so fine, and so beautiful that I wanted to shout something, but didn't know what. And I knew it was all transient. Even if I could sit there for ever, listening, taking deep breaths and looking for young colors, I couldn't hold it by knowing it.

I saw Jack, coming across the campus toward me. She paced a little faster.

I had a strange thought: what if *this* is the happiest moment in my life? I felt good, I felt happy, and there was someone special coming toward me. It will all change and decay and I'll never feel this good again.

I threw that out because it was spoiling my vision.

Jill used to turn her head a little when she saw me, as if to signal to anyone watching that there was nothing between us – true enough most of the time. Elaine used to stop dead still and resume at a snail's pace, waiting for *me* to hurry toward *her*. Oh, and long ago . . . Sharon. Sharon never saw me until I stepped on her toes. Maybe she needed glasses. Odd to think that Sharon is now twenty-six, and where is she now? She was only nineteen when we met. My first girlfriend, and I spent most of the time drunk on my ass. That's when I discovered that bedding young women, trying to study, and a lot of liquor didn't work out well. I lost my financial aid for a year because of my grade point average.

Who is this Jack that I let her come walking toward me so certainly? What's she doing to me? When I want to be alone, there she is, or there I am thinking about her.

This morning, we woke up kissing. I don't even know who started it because we were both asleep, muzzy and cool. I liked watching her wake slowly. Later, she sat and watched me make coffee, just sitting there, quietly smiling and yawning.

I had asked her what she was going to tell her parents.

'I'm going to tell them the truth. I'm not a very good liar. Don't worry, I won't give them your address or anything.'

'Good. I would hate the police to show up at my place in the middle of the night.'

'Oh. My father doesn't care enough to do something like that. He just goes through the motions of being a father. He gets things to use on me later, to make me feel guilty.'

'He's probably not that bad,' I said. I was thinking that she sounded so young when she talked about her parents, still showing signs of adolescent rebellion. But I heard something more in her words – a terrible pain. I couldn't stand to learn much more than that. I wanted to sit and just *listen* to her then but we had to leave so she could make it to her first class.

We had a few minutes together again, when I was feeling so good. We walked. Everyone seemed tranquilly drugged by the pure spring air. Faces stared out of the old windows of the sandstone buildings enviously. This wasn't the day to think of Einstein or the founding of Jamestown, or cost accounting. It was a day to turn blue and green with the sky and grass.

I laughed and Jack looked at me.

'I feel good,' I said, because I wanted her to know that she was part of the reason for it.

She grinned.

Suddenly, someone very strong was intruding on me. I was distracted by the familiar, but new, shape of the personality nearby. I looked around. I didn't know anyone, and couldn't put a face or name to the person that I sensed. Who was it? – like a song you can't quite remember the lyrics to . . .

I stopped. Two men stepped out of the Social Science building, speaking politely to each other.

I strained toward them, watching. They didn't seem to know each other well, but they walked slowly and talked about important business. They were finished with a deal, and both satisfied.

'Hi, Jack,' one of them said.

'Hi.' She sounded a little shy, flattered to be noticed.

I fell out of step with her. I knew exactly who the other man was – it was the umbrella man. My heart stopped. All the air in my lungs became hard. Only my mind was moving. The man stared right at me, right into me, and he was gentle, keen, curious. He recognized me somehow, yes, he knew me. Or perhaps it was because I stared at him, panicking. He looked at me, then at Jack. I made myself take a step. I turned away then – I didn't want it to show that I had seen and known.

'Kolya?'

That was it. Jack said my name. He knew what he needed to know and walked away with the other man.

All this in just seconds. I see it again and again in my mind and I know that he will find me again somehow. I will never walk this path again. I will take the snow tunnels. I have to get through this somehow and get away. I know that he recognized me and will find me. Oh, God, oh, God!

'What's the matter with you?' Jack asked.

'He knew me.'

'What?'

I forced myself to walk, but my heart pounded so hard that I thought I would topple. I turned to look. The umbrella man and his companion were walking away. I had never seen either of them before.

'Do you know that man?'

'What man?'

I nodded toward them. 'The one on the left, with the dark hair. Not the one who spoke to you.'

Jack squinted. 'No, I don't recognize him. He's with Dr Klein, the department chairman.'

'Of?'

'Psychology.'

'Oh.'

'I'm going to be late for class,' she said. 'See you later.'

I stood outside and shivered, then caught the bus home.

Nicholas Alexandrovich Dal.

Nicholas Alexandrovich Dal.

Son of Alexander Fyodorovich, son of Fyodor Nicholaevich, son of . . .

Does it matter? Why do we do it? Count backward as far as we can, look at the people scattering more DNA that will go out and scatter more DNA.

Isn't it strange that we came out of the sea and we can't go back? I could never live by the sea; it would swallow me.

13 March

I waited in the hallway, looking for Jack. It seemed that thousands shuffled by, some urgently, some slowly, and I had glimpses of the tops of dark-haired heads, but no Jack. Five minutes until class. I got a garbled reading of the people in the building, but no Jack.

Then she tapped me on the shoulder as I lit a cigarette. I jumped.

'What'cha doin'?' she asked playfully.

'Waiting for you.'

'You look like you need some sleep.'

'Yeah.' I didn't know what to say now. I leaned against the wall. I felt awful. 'I have to ask you something and I don't want you to take it the wrong way.'

'Okay, ask me.' She looked worried, though her mouth tried to be cheerful.

'Someone's after me. I think he can trace me through you now. I want you to stay away from my house for at least a week.'

'Oh.' She was puzzled and hurt. She couldn't help but take it the wrong way, I could see that.

'It's not you,' I said as gently as I could. I really didn't want her feelings hurt. I put my hand on her shoulder. 'I hate to ask you this, and I know what it sounds like, but believe me, I can't risk it. It's just a personal family thing.'

'But why would someone be after you?'

'We've always had problems like this, being immigrants.'

'You're not an immigrant,' she said.

'Close enough. There were some problems in my family before grandfather and grandmother came over.'

She smiled. 'Are you Commie spies?'

'No, that's not funny. Well, yes, it is funny,' I said,

smiling back at her. How she can bounce back. I wish I were that elastic. 'Actually, I would probably be happiest in a Greek tyranny, how's that for politics? That's not true, either, but I'm apolitical. I see too many sides to things.'

'Kolya, are you all right?'

'Well,' I said, knowing that I couldn't hide it, 'I do have a bit of a hangover today.'

I had gone home yesterday, found Gus trying to return my bicycle, and we'd had a few together. We played chess and talked about revolution and marriage. Rather, Gus had talked; I listened. 'Goddamn, Kolya, I've spilled my guts to you again,' Gus said.

'What kind of problems did your family have – in Russia?' she asked.

'I'll tell you some time.' Already, I'd said too much. But it really mattered to me that she didn't think I was cutting her off. I had to tell her something, and I'm not good at lying.

'Are you sure you aren't being paranoid?'

'No!' I said. An old reflex, I couldn't help but feel the sharp slap of the word. 'I'm not paranoid – about this.' I flipped my cigarette into the bin. 'That's all I wanted to say.'

She stood, eyes down. I regretted the tone I'd just used, but couldn't bring myself to apologize. Then she looked back up at me. 'And after a week, what then?'

'I don't know.'

'Do you want me to leave you alone? Have I already messed up our deal?' she asked.

Solitude. Just me, the moon, and my shadow. I touched her hair. Her hair and her eyes and the way she's made inside. I like Jack a lot; more than I should. I had always imagined feeling this way about a fellow (female) vagabond more like myself, living somewhere on the edge of life as most people live it. Another cowering wreck, scuttling through events and occupations, feeling for ever the out-sider. But here she is, with her happy childhood, her good sense, her stable outlook, her resilience. I think I envy her.

Could she bring me a little light from the 'real' world, just so I can understand a little better what's going on?

But now, I wonder – what am I going to do to her? What good could it possibly do for her to be leading demons by the hand, wherever she went?

And as I looked at her, hesitating over the words, her eyes filled. She turned away. 'I've tried to be honest . . . '

'All right, I'll tell you,' I said. How can I tell her what I don't know? Do I want her, do I want to be left alone? If only I could have both. 'Don't go,' I said, 'we'll figure something out. I want to keep seeing you, Jack.'

She smiled, her eyes filled a little more. She walked abruptly into the classroom.

I sat across from her. She didn't look at me. She drew blue circles around the holes in her notebook paper. When Dr Estes came in, we learned about Charles the First. I couldn't really pay much attention. I was feeling confused and sad, then I realized that Jack was feeling that, too. Eventually, I shut her out, and concentrated wholly on Dr Estes's lecture.

I don't know a match from an atom bomb. I'm in trouble.

After class, we walked slowly toward the stairway. Here we had to part, me to chemistry in the Science building and Jack to human paleontology in the Social Science building. We stopped about halfway down the steps. I was thinking. I wanted to talk to her about many things; she might have some interesting answers. But just a little at a time. 'Have you taken psychology courses?' I asked her.

'It's my minor.'

'Oh.' So Dr Klein probably knows her last name as well. He had known her first name when he'd greeted her yesterday. But then, it is easy to remember Jack's. 'Is Dr Klein pretty good? He teaches . . . what?'

'I had him for Abnormal Psych. One and Two. Yeah, he's pretty good, except he has others lecture for him a lot. An important person, always going to meetings or something.'

'What do you think of things like extrasensory perception?'

She shrugged. We were at the bottom of the steps now, and students still streamed around us. The cavernous stairwell echoed dozens of footfalls per second. We walked outside. The sunlight shone on her hair and in her eyes. She looked a little forlorn, hugging her books against her.

'I really don't know. I read more against than in favor, of course, but you can't help but think something might be possible. In the Soviet Union, they've stopped asking whether it really exists or not, and just go on researching as if it does.'

'Yeah.'

We looked at each other. I saw a familiar look about her, this look of wanting me. I wished that I had some place underground or in the air, or underwater – safe and far away – to take her for several hours and just kiss her and look at her.

'I'd better go to class,' I said.

'Yeah, me too.' She tried to smile. She hesitated, then said, 'Oh, Kolya, I don't know what I'd do without you to talk to. You're so understanding. You're so . . . ' She leaned into my shoulder and, for a moment, I thought she would cry, but she turned away from me suddenly and started off.

' 'Bye,' I said.

Part of the way across the campus, over a small ridge, beyond a small hedge, I had a terrible pang of missing her. But, when I turned to look, I couldn't see her any more.

14 March

I couldn't make it through the day without her. I went down to the liquor store and called her house from the phone booth there. The Awful Father answered the phone, but he didn't really sound like an ogre at all. More like someone's father. Jack came to the phone. She had just been reading, she said, and no, I wasn't bothering her. What a silly question, she said. I asked her if she would like to meet me somewhere and we could go for a drive in the mountains. It was still nice weather, and several hours of sunshine were left. I would bring the cheese and wine, and she could bring the blanket.

I rode my bicycle to a busy intersection and waited for her truck. She pulled in; I loaded the bicycle and told her to drive wherever she liked. We passed the spot by the creek that I go to sometimes, but I didn't even look at it as we passed. Not yet. She pointed to an old road, and said she used to go up there when she was a kid. Some of it was the edge of a national forest, or public land of some sort so it wouldn't be trespassing, and there would be no park fee. We drove up the road, dust flying everywhere like orange foam, and parked near a stand of spruce. It was still warm and bright. We walked, carrying the blanket. I had actually brought some cheese and apples and wine. She had a canteen of water. Water! She can seem so spartan sometimes.

As we walked, I felt far from town, the only sounds our breathing, our feet crunching in the sandy soil and dry needles. I made love to her a hundred times in my mind as we made our way, imagining it this way and that, savoring how it would be in just a few moments. I thought I would explode if she didn't find a place that suited her soon.

Finally, on a rise, thick with old trees, scratchy brush, we kicked a few rocks away and spread the blanket. We attacked each other. It was the most aggressive I've ever been, and I was sober, too. It was almost frightening. Out there, completely alone, filled with her, filled with the stillness of evening in the woods, I felt animal-like. Nothing cerebral at all about the way we squeezed and grunted and bit. It wasn't just me, either, she answered it all. She brought the universe crashing down and rearranged me.

I sensed something in her. I was so close to her, I knew how she felt about me. It was scary. I've never looked in

75

that mirror before. Her Kolya is wise, mysterious, passionate, and just a little mad. I felt it all. I was inside and outside her, and she surrounded me.

Oh, hell, oh, damnation, oh generations of curse . . . I thought of my mother. I hated my father for letting me in on his lovemaking with Miranda all those years, and I was angry with myself that I couldn't help but remember this as I made love to someone that I really care about.

But I got rid of that. Jack, Jack, Susanna Pavlovna, she is mine!

It's better first hand.

We lay on the blanket until nearly dark, eating a little cheese, drinking a little wine, talking about ordinary things – games we used to play as children, books we've read, movies we've seen. Jack told me about some of the places she's been to – New Mexico, Texas, even Juarez, Mexico. It all sounds so strange to me, as I have never been further away than Gunnison.

When I got home this evening, I thought about Miranda again, and wondered why my father had even married her. She whined and complained and was dull, predictable.

I decided to go out and call Papa. As I walked, I thought about him. I used to probe him endlessly, always staying near, always tuned to him. All through dinner, and then even as he lay in bed with my mother. He never told me not to, and Papa has amazing sensitivity. He knew when either Grandfather or I were checking him out. He used to send me signals and we'd never look at each other, rarely say a word. It drove Miranda crazy because she knew something was going on. She could never find the wires that connected us. Once in a while, when I was feeling his feelings, he'd look up at me and smile, as if having someone crawl around inside his head and heart was a pleasure.

Papa can share himself. I never learned that. But it wasn't his fault. I think it was because of Miranda. I used to be afraid of him catching me hating her, then loving her, then thinking about how they felt when they made love.

Dr Wall used to say sly things about Miranda to me. He

thought I had an Oedipal complex, I'm sure. It's because of her that I never screwed anyone while sober. Maybe I was afraid that when I opened my eyes she would be there. Like today, thinking about her . . . This isn't the regular Oedipus, though, is it? I never really wanted her, I just accidentally had her because of the way my family is. And that was my sexual experience from the time I was zero until I was a pretty big boy.

She was like a wife to me because I was in my father's heart so much. In return, I never got that love back. She saw me as the reason for everything that was wrong. I was safety because I was to blame for everything. She made a mistake though. She underestimated that man she called 'Alex' who was really someone named Sasha.

If only she had known what a foul thing she'd birthed, if only Papa had told her everything, if only I had never been conceived . . .

I will never let it happen again. It's a great sense of accomplishment to me that I will never have children, that I have put an end to all of this.

I got to the phone and talked to Papa for a while about his job, my school. I told him that I had found a girlfriend, and he was glad. We started talking about women a little and I asked him why he had loved Miranda.

'Because she gave me you,' he said without hesitation. Then he added, 'And she never asked questions.'

Poor Papa. He'll never find another like that.

16 March

This week, we have been meeting on campus earlier every day and staying later between classes. I was late to every class for three days this week. The weather was almost hot this afternoon. I saw students carrying tennis rackets with their books, but right now, at 2 a.m., it is snowing again. I'm getting tired of the snow, but I think that every spring when there are enough days to remind me of early summer.

Today, Jack was wearing a shirt of silky material, short sleeves, low neck. I could hardly keep from staring at her chest. She seemed a little depressed; we hadn't talked about what we would do after today and next week is spring break. I had things in mind, but hadn't mentioned them yet. She has become much more tentative than that first week, when she nearly moved in with me. Now she keeps her distance until I make a move.

She told me that her mother is doing better, but her father is worse. 'She's getting used to being at home. I guess I'm not as worried about her right now because she seems okay. But you should see my father straining to make everything perfect. It's like we're all on stage all the time. Last night, Mom asked if we had half-and-half for coffee. Julie got up and looked in the fridge. We were out. Simple. Nobody thought to buy any. Well, Mom has always liked half-and-half instead of milk, but she never *had* to have it. She said, "Oh, I have to watch my figure anyway," and Dad started to shout at Julie for not getting the half-and-half.'

I wondered what the point was, and why such a trivial argument would upset her so.

'You should have seen the way Mom looked at him. Really strange,' she said. She paused and stared at the memory. 'I've never seen a look like that on her face. Kind of like she was sick of us all. I felt weird. Why should she be angry with us? We didn't give her cancer.' Jack bit her lip. 'I didn't mean that. That was terrible.'

'And what did Honest Jack say to her?' I asked.

Jack frowned. It was a long time before she looked back at me. 'I can't.'

'Can't?'

'Dad told me that if I upset her, if I say one single thing to make her think about being sick, that I'll be on my own. I couldn't finish school.'

God almighty, I thought, what a mess. They were tangling each other up no end. 'Don't you have moments when you could talk to her privately? You could explain to her that you didn't want your father to think you were upsetting her, and not to mention it.'

'I never really have a chance. He's there when I'm there. She's gone during the day a lot. I don't know where she goes, but as soon as she felt better, she started going out during the day. I think she just goes shopping or something, because she's gotten us some new clothes.'

'Like this?' I touched the silky blouse. 'I like your mother's taste.'

Jack smiled vaguely. 'Yeah.'

'I thought you had tons of money in the bank.'

'That money's for Europe,' she said anxiously.

I felt that she was desperately torn. Guilt.

'It's not tons of money, anyway,' she said. 'I have this awful feeling, Kolya, that I'm more important because she's not going to be around. I will be, and this is my only chance to go. I don't want to miss it. I hate myself for that.'

'Your family is a mess.' I squeezed her shoulders. She was close to tears but I didn't want her to cry. I wasn't being affected by her pain because I'd had a beer at lunch. Just sensitive enough to know what she was feeling, but safe. I would have been knocked down by her mood otherwise.

'Well, look,' I said, trying to make a joke. 'I owe you some money. I'll give it back to you if you need it because you talked to your mother and will miss Rome.'

She looked stricken.

'No, I don't mean for you to give the key back. But I'll do what I can to help, okay?'

She nodded. She leaned against me and I patted her back. 'I . . . ' she started but never finished.

'You're not an awful person. These are bad times, that's all.'

'Have you heard any more about the person looking for you?' she asked.

'No.'

'Oh.'

79

'Why don't we see each other tomorrow anyway? I'll give you a call. Or listen, come over after dark. Drive around for a while. Make sure no one is following you. Then park in the next block and walk around. Would you like to come and stay with me?' I chucked her chin.

She laughed. 'Who's after you, CIA or KGB?'

'I don't know,' I said.

'Should I carry a weapon? I have a Swiss army knife. If the blade is dull, I'll stick the corkscrew in their eyes.' She made a stabbing gesture in the air.

We laughed. Jack's instructor walked by, smiling serenely at his tardy student. Subdued, Jack followed him into the classroom, with a secret smile over her shoulder for me.

22 March

Not much to say about this week so far. I've gotten a lot of homework done. Read Gene Smith's book on President Wilson, some E.B. White and Welty short stuff, and *Lost Horizon*. I wonder if a perfect place ever really could accommodate imperfect people? There are those who are stubbornly wayward, ultimately malleable by goodness. But what of those who cannot change?

What would I be in Shangri-La? Still a misfit.

I prefer to cling to the edges of things, choosing the good and the bad for myself, watching from my side. The beautiful and right life, no matter what version, is for others.

Lost Horizon leaves me depressed, detached. I pity the sweetness of the characters, and feel emptiness in what others find inspiring.

Now, I am finally going to re-read *The Idiot*. Prince Mishkin, now *there* is a human being!

Saw Jack last two nights. We drove to Central City and had a beer in a sleazy old tavern filled with local drunks.

The mountains are peaceful and cold. We just talked. It was good.

She would be happy in Shangri-La. It disturbs me.

30 March

As soon as I got to work today, Patricia asked me about my summer schedule. Summer, already? She must have just come out of the ladies' room where she douses herself with perfume because I could hardly breathe around her. But, she's always thinking of me, always giving me first choice at things. I don't know why I even notice her faults because she is so good-hearted. Perhaps she is especially kind to me because there aren't many library science students at the university. I told her once, facetiously, that I couldn't imagine anything better than spending the rest of my life looking through indexes of fine print, showing people how catalogs work, and looking up the length of the Nile. She took me seriously, patting my shoulder, and told me I was a little idealistic. She said there was more to it, but I would do all right.

I scratched my head and made a 'mm' at her when she asked me about my schedule. Patricia doesn't like direct answers. If I look thoughtful for a few seconds, then she feels some effort has been made.

'Let's see,' I said. 'It seems to me that I could work full-time this summer, and take evening classes. Yes, maybe I'll do that.'

'I don't want you to have any problems with classes. You've been working so hard this year.'

'Can you use me during the day, Patricia?' I asked.

'Well, if you really want that, I'll put it on my tentative schedule. All right?'

'Thank you.'

She went away and I could breathe again. I left the desk for a few moments. I needed to find some books to write a term paper. Someone, probably someone named Susanne Elizabeth Berdo, has taken most of the books on the Plantagenets. I found a book on King John. Do I want to invest twenty pages on King John? No. But I couldn't think of anything else. I had thought, perversely, of writing an attack on Richard the Third.

I went back to the desk empty-handed. I decided to put it off. I just didn't know what to write about.

As soon as I settled back down, Patricia came by. She was carrying a book. 'Just got this out of Technical Services. You might be interested. It's about Wat Tyler and the Peasant Revolt of 1381.' She put the book in my hands. 'Maybe you could do your term paper on *that*.'

'Thank you,' I said, a little mystified. I really couldn't recall saying a single word about my English history class. A thought occurred to me – perhaps Patricia is a telepath. A telepath would have the same problems as we do. Putting up a pleasant front to fend off bad readings is Papa's way of handling things, too – always smiling, friendly. I almost laughed aloud, watching her walk back through the stacks.

Maybe libraries are filled with people who have special talents.

I began to read the book. It is interesting enough that I have decided this will be my topic. It got close to five o'clock and I heard someone call my name.

Elaine. Tall, fluffy-haired, slinky body, perfect teeth. Emotionally bland. One of my compromise situations: dull but easy to be with. I hadn't seen her all semester.

'Hi,' I said.

'Howya been?'

I closed the Wat Tyler book. 'All right. And you?'

'Been looking for you. Didn't you take Classical Civ. a few semesters back?'

'Last spring.'

'Who'd you have?'

'Mendoza.'

'What did you do your paper on?'

'Alexandria's library.'

'Of course.' She made a ha-ha sound, not a laugh but a flatulent smile which I had once been rather fond of, but it wore thin. 'May I borrow your paper?'

'How closely are you going to borrow?'

'Oh, not much. Not enough so anyone would recognize it. I'll do my paper on Alexandria, a little less specific. The library bit is boring anyway.'

'I guess that's all right,' I said. 'I'll bring it with me here next week.'

'Oh. I was going to write it over the weekend.'

I looked at her. I was curious; she didn't really care that much about the paper. It was something else. Yes, exactly. She's in need of a little attention, I realized. I didn't want to be the one to give it to her. That had been used up in me long ago.

'I'll bring it by sometime this weekend. Are you still in the same place?'

'Yeah, but why don't I give you a lift home? I still have the bike rack on my car.'

I shrugged, not wanting to argue about details, when, where. I would simply give her the paper and make her go away. 'I've moved further from campus.'

'Oh, why's that?'

I began to clear up business for the day, putting pens away, filing tally sheets. 'Found a nice place.'

'Yeah? Need a roommate?'

'No. You rebounding, Elaine?' I laughed.

'You haven't changed,' she said, smiling. She reached across the desk and tousled my hair, something else that I'd once liked and eventually found annoying. Cute.

And wrong. I saw someone familiar move by just at that moment. It was Jack – headed into the stacks. I replayed what had just transpired from the point of view of someone standing at the doors – me laughing, pretty Elaine romping in my hair. I knew it had chilled Jack.

I shot away from the desk and hurried across the library. I could still see her, but she was too far away to call out to.

'Jack,' I said.

She turned her head a little. I know she saw me. She made a quick dash for the ladies' room. I stopped and stared at the door helplessly.

To hell with her, I thought. To hell with them all. Let her think what she wants. Who is she anyway? I never made a single promise to her about anything like this. She was just weighing me down anyway.

I walked back. Elaine still waited at the circulation desk, without a trace of impatience or care. She leaned against the desk, twisting her foot on her toes casually. She wore a skirt that showed her legs and also the shape of her rear. I thought, in a moment of reaction, that it would be nice to drill her while sober. Maybe I'd made too much of Jack being so special because I hadn't been drunk every time.

I tried not to show how changed I felt to Elaine. 'Let's go,' I said, picking up my books. 'Leaving!' I called to Patricia. 'I think there's someone in the ladies' room.'

She nodded and waved.

We hooked my bicycle onto her small car. I got inside and was amazed at how familiar it all was, even though I hadn't been with her for a long time. We both noticed the bad weather coming on suddenly. I tried to think of something light, terribly cynical and funny to say, but actually I was sinking into a mire of regret. I should have waited for Jack to come out; I should have told Elaine to go away; I should never have spoken to women at all . . .

I gave her instructions on driving to my house, a few blocks at a time.

'Now, wait a minute, Nicholas, I've turned east three times, north once, then south. What goes?'

I had forgotten Elaine's spatial ability. She is, after all, an architecture major. 'I like the scenic route,' I said.

'I'll never understand you.' She was amused by me, but she wasn't really irritated.

'Most likely.'

She pulled up in the carport. I unhooked my bicycle and locked it in the carport storage shed. Elaine walked around the house, peering at the front and back.

'It seems so suburban for you.'

We went inside. 'Like something to drink?' I asked her.

'No, thanks.' She sat down in the rocking chair. 'You even have furniture, I see. You've changed your lifestyle.'

'Not really. It's an illusion.' I squatted by my desk and looked through a box of file folders and pulled one out for her. 'Here you go.'

'Hey, thanks. You're a pal.' She opened the folder and flipped through it, sitting so naturally and comfortably in my living room, as if she'd been there many times.

'Return it,' I said.

'Sure.' She dropped it onto the floor and stood, looking around the house a little more. She went into the bedroom and looked at the mattresses on the floor. 'Same old Kolya,' she said. She began to undress, first kicking off her shoes, then pulling her blouse out from the waist of her skirt.

'Hop in, 'Lane,' I said, standing at the door. 'Don't mind me.' I was irritated that she didn't even ask or try to seduce me.

'Oh, come on, what's the matter?' she asked. 'Aren't we old friends?'

Come on, I told myself, what's the matter with you, indeed? She was lovely, somehow all tanned and sleek and summery even at this time of year. She was down to her panties, and I started to unbutton my shirt. She peeled completely and stretched out on the mattress. I sat down and took my shoes off. She put her arms around me from behind.

'You getting it regularly from somewhere else?' she asked.

I couldn't help but sense everything in her and felt revulsion. I couldn't even define what it is about her, but she is so different from me, so predatory in such a casual way. I was repelled by her because she suddenly seemed so cold. I tried kissing her, but was distracted. Her personality gripped me as strongly as if I'd told her an embarrassing secret and she had laughed at me.

It would never work.

I got up. 'Need a drink.'

'Oh, hell,' she said, 'I forgot to ask you if you'd done that, Cossack.'

I gritted my teeth.

When I got into the kitchen, I took a long drink. I lingered, even taking down a glass and pouring, rather than drinking from the bottle. I began to imagine a chain of events. I looked out the window, down the street. The sun was still shining, but sideways, raking the land, and heavy clouds rolled in over the mountains. What if Patricia is a telepath and she has been 'reading' me all along, and the entire faculty of the psychology department knows about it, and they are co-operating with the umbrella man? I don't know any of them, always avoided the entire department, classes, students, and all. Maybe Elaine had been contacted because Patricia knew Elaine used to come around and pick me up all the time. And Jack was part of it, too. She was running from me because she was really just checking to see that Elaine was doing her job. Elaine had been so calculating, so insistent. Why now? Why today?

I checked the front door and windows to see that everything was locked up, then walked to the bedroom.

'Are you plotting against me?' I asked Elaine, thinking that the direct approach would throw her off balance.

She laughed. Salty, dry, barren bitch with perfect teeth. I hated her. I stripped off my jeans and fucked her. She still looked expectant but I was absolutely finished.

'Go on. Please go home.'

'Gladly,' she said, dressing. 'You're getting worse. I'd forgotten how unpleasant you can be.'

I didn't move after she left. I felt like crying, but just lay there until after dark. I thought vaguely about getting up to check the door, but after all that, I didn't care if they came and got me. What could they take from me now, anyway?

It's snowing again. I think I feel better at this moment, but am still feeling down.

31 March

I remember being surprised when I woke up in my own room this morning. But the mood that I held then has evaporated after today.

I decided to go to the Denver Public Library, just to get away. There was a chance that they would have a book on Wat Tyler, too, though it was doubtful they would have anything the university doesn't have. I caught the bus early.

Only the north shadows still had a powdering of snow. The sky was bright and cool. The smog was nearly gone for the weekend. It reminded me of the way Denver had been when I was young, a small, intelligent city with a pretty backdrop of blue-purple mountains. But the stretches of condominiums, industrial parks, and shopping centers that I could see from the bus, coming into the city, depressed me as usual.

Inside the library, it is always the same – smelling of old books, bound magazines, paper, ink. Unhurried movement, self-absorbed people shuffling and rustling, the occasional whirr of the pneumatic tubes. I love that library. I rarely have to go hiding from people there; I can stand with others in the stacks, muttering 'excuse me' and crossing on. I like to walk along and touch the varnished grain on the old heavy tables; I like to hear the hollow cry the chairs make when scooted on linoleum.

I spent one summer, probably at the age of thirteen or fourteen, giving myself a complete tour of the library. I started with the lowest numbers and looked at every title on the shelves. I like to walk from section to section, looking at the local history displays, perusing free folders, special exhibits. I like to sit near a desk and listen to the librarians, the questions they answer over the phone, the conversations they have with each other, the way they speak so nicely to people who don't know a book from a biscuit.

So many books! Not just the academic volumes sitting on college shelves: *How to Fold Paper Airplanes*, *Your Career as a Civil Servant*, *A Model Talks to Teenage Girls*, *Learn*

Yiddish, *Flower Arrangement*, *Build a Patio*, and *Build a Better Vocabulary Through Newspapers*. What a full life one could have if it were possible to read all these little tomes of self-improvement and enlightenment!

I was wandering slowly toward the twelfth century when I passed through the medical and psychology section. (Though I avoid these people, I know their books.) And there, holding a book in both palms, stood a woman that I knew.

She was fragile and silver-haired. She was beautiful, and I had no trouble recognizing her.

I hesitated. What would I say to her? But I was drawn. I strolled over to the row she stood in and pretended to look at the books near her. She glanced at my shoulder, my position, but not at my face, and looked back at her book.

Kübler-Ross. She was reading about dying in the anonymous stacks of the public library in a city hours from her house. My heart was pounding; I felt weak in her presence.

I was sinking. No, she was sunken. I had to speak, but I was getting low.

How could she stand there so calmly and feel like this? I was sick with dread and started to move away before she crippled me.

Then she looked up at my face.

We stared at each other. I tried to smile, but I was shrinking. I felt I would have her voice when I opened my mouth, but instead, my voice said, 'Susanne Berdo?'

She snapped the book shut and tucked it under her arm. 'Who are you?'

'Nicholas Dal.'

She looked puzzled.

'Kolya,' I said.

'Oh!' She nodded.

'I recognized you from a picture.' And saying that, I remembered all the feelings I had experienced looking at her picture. They were still there, intact, but now I was haunted by her gestures, her voice and smell as well. Her eyes expressed a flatness, and opened only to look upon the world as a courtesy, or safety. She seemed to me to have that autumness of a pressed leaf, partly because she had a slight yellowish tinge to her complexion.

She wanted me to go. She felt trapped by me standing here, intruding on the time she had to herself. I knew this feeling. It is mine, too, in other cases.

'Well, nice meeting you,' I said, half-wanting just to sit and watch her from a distance. But I needed to get a drink of water.

'Yes,' she said. 'You should come to the house some-time.'

'I will.' I whispered because of where we were, and because I was weakening.

She was consumed with horror and I, fascinated like one reading a frightening story, was consumed with her horror, too. She meshed with me so easily that I could almost feel the impression of the book she held in her hands on my palms.

'Kolya,' she said suddenly, 'you won't tell them that you saw me here?'

'If you won't tell anyone that you saw me,' I said. We are both refugees. I smiled.

She smiled.

I felt a change; the grip lessened, but I backed away from her.

'Did you see what I was reading?' she asked, then held the book up to me. I read the words *On Death and Dying* unwillingly, as if she were showing me something obscene.

I nodded. I couldn't speak to her. My cells were drumming. I was getting parched inside. 'Susanne,' I started, then realized that I'd presumed in calling her by her first name, but she only looked down at the cover of the book sadly.

I saw her quiver.

Inside that flesh crawls death – inexorable, painful, and real. We all die some day, but Susanne's some day is rushing at her while she watches. She needs to talk. Good God, I came here and found her, and of all the people in the world, I am the one she will talk to. She didn't push me away any longer. I had, through a smile, changed my role of intruder.

'Shall we go outside?' I knew that I needed cool air.

She nodded, little jerks of her head up and down. She didn't look at me, simply shelved the book and waited for me to lead her.

We walked through the library cautiously. I felt that any bump or sudden noise would shatter her, she was so tightly strung. Outside, there was no place to sit, so we stood on the sidewalk, both of us staring vacantly across the street at the shiny, mud-colored tiles of the art museum, a building that looks like the dream of a bathroom designer gone glorious. I lit a cigarette with shaking hands.

I didn't know what to say to her. I almost said something about the weather. She was quiet. She sparked suddenly. 'I need to put a dime in the meter.'

We walked across the lawn to her car parked at the curb. She put a coin in the meter, then leaned against the fender of her car. Then she pulled herself up and sat on the fender, which surprised me. She seemed so light, lithe, and young, somehow, like a teenager. The yellow, red, and blue flowers on her loose embroidered blouse that she wore over jeans were so alive and vivid.

'Will Jack's hair be like yours some day?' I asked, breaking our silence.

Susanne touched her hair self-consciously. 'Probably.'

'It's very pretty.'

'That's sweet,' she said, and I felt like a child.

I smoked and looked away from her.

'May I have a cigarette?' she asked. 'I haven't had one in years. Paul and I quit so we wouldn't get lung cancer.'

I took a cigarette out and lit it for her with my own. I didn't want to hold a match for her; she would see me tremble. 'Do you come to Denver often?' I asked, re-membering Jack saying that her mother went out a lot.

'Yes, sometimes. It's my secret life. I don't know how much you know . . . '

90

'I know a lot,' I said. I sat on the fender next to her. I couldn't look at her directly; she absorbed me with those eyes.

'My family is pretending that nothing is happening to me, so I have to go somewhere and let it be really happening.' She took a deep drag on the cigarette. 'Makes me dizzy. Do you want it?' She held the cigarette out.

I shook my head. She dropped it in the gutter, which was trickling with melted snow.

'But why should I drag them all into hell with me? Especially Julie. Julie has no defenses. She has no idea of what's really going on. Oh, she knows. But she doesn't *realize*.'

'That's not your fault,' I said.

'Oh, it must be. I've been exiled, punished.'

'Oh, no. They don't know what to say to you. If only you knew how Jack feels.'

Susanne bowed her head, picked at nubs on her jeans.

'Maybe you should try talking to them one by one. It might be easier than at the dinner table. Start with Jack. I don't see how you could fail to get Jack to talk.'

'They run from me!' she said loudly. 'I'm either alone completely or with all of them at once, ever since I got home from the hospital. They're afraid of me.' She made fists. 'Of *me*. Afraid of me,' she said in disbelief.

I put my arm around her when she began to weep. She leaned against me. I was so lonely, and so reassured. I was frightened. My throat ached. I stroked her hair, which was soft for grey hair, not like Grandmama's wiry grey. I held her closer. I had to cough or weep with her. Afraid, but with someone near me. Someone listens to me. Pour it out.

And then I was angry. It was so unfair.

'Thing is . . . ' she said, her voice piping. 'I could still live on for a long time – who knows? Six months, a year. I could. That's such a long time to be walking through walls and having people look through you.'

I loosened my hold on her, looking at her face.

'Paul has already buried me. I've been dead for weeks.'

Remembering how those flowers on her clothes, the brightness of her movements and voice had disturbed me, I went cold. Susanne was more alive than dead. I, too, had made her a ghost, given her an ethereal quality. She was real.

'You see me,' she said.

'Yes, now I do. I know what's happened.'

'I thought . . .' She laughed, still looking at me. 'For a moment I was thinking . . .'

'What?' I asked, but I knew that neither of us would talk about it. Something was there.

'I don't want to leave,' she said, wistfully, now gazing across the lawn of the library. The Saturday traffic moved slowly down Broadway. I smelled bus exhaust, listening to her more calmly now. 'I don't want to leave my daughters,' she said. 'I'll never know what happens to them.' She took a tissue out of her purse and blew her nose. 'I wish that I could have grown up now, like Jack. She's lucky, being a woman now. I wish that I could see how it all turns out, but I'll never know.'

I took her hand.

'They'll forget me.'

'How could they?'

'What will they remember me by? I'm not leaving a trace of myself behind except for them.'

I shook my head, unable to think of comfort.

'I'll be dead . . . dead . . . dead.' She said it with different inflections as if to test the reality of the word. 'I'm dying. I'm not going to exist at this time next year. It's so strange. I didn't believe it for a while, I thought there had been a mistake. But now I feel it – move over, Susanne, it says, I'm taking you a piece at a time and the doctors can't cut that fast or far. I try to sleep at night, I try to touch my husband, but he moves away. He won't touch me because I'm dead, and contaminated with death. He washes things after I've handled them. He throws food away if I take a bite or sip of it. It must be awful to have a dead person in your bed at night, still clawing at you when you'd rather roll over and forget.'

I was frozen. I couldn't move. I burned and froze, fascinated and sick. My bones rattled inside me. I could hear ticking inside my eardrums.

'Sometimes I think trying to live is worse than dying. I think I'll give it up.'

She looked at me but I was still. 'I see that I've said enough. Thank you, I am sorry that you had to listen to all this.'

She dropped lightly to the ground and walked into the library without glancing back at me.

When I could move, I walked across the street to the art museum and threw up in the men's room. I got to Grandmama's, she put me to bed and brought me hot tea.

I looked in the mirror for a long time this evening when I got home.

Who is it?

My bathroom: a water glass of vodka, a slimy soap dish with blue scum, a small pair of scissors for trimming the hairs on my face. A brush with brown hairs tangled in the bristles. A toothbrush. Toothpaste. Deodorant.

I looked at these things and I was Richard the Third or Nicholas the Umpth. If I were a king, having done away with the rest of my family because I wanted to be the *only one left*, the historians of Century Futuretimes would study the things that I touch every day, trying to draw the essence of the madman out of a single strand of coarse brown hair, a smear of toothpaste on porcelain, the scent of my soap.

His heart was broken by others. What was he thinking about when he washed the guilty face?

Mad Nicholas Alexandrovich spat here.

2 April

This is how I remember it.

After drinking most of the evening when I got home, I

had trouble getting the door open. A terrible time lag in what I wanted to do and could do, I was so drunk. I expected the umbrella man and was going to fall into his arms, but it was Papa.

'Alexander Fyodorovich! Come in! The Tsar's been expecting you for dinner. Did you bring your remarkable family? We've heard so much about them.' I thought it was funny, but he didn't laugh.

Papa stepped in tentatively. He wore a threadbare flannel shirt and workpants. A baker that looks like a piece of dough wrapped in rags.

'Last time I saw you, you were drinking. Have you taken a break?' he asked. He turned on a light.

'No, Papa, I've been drunk for a solid month.' I sat down on the floor and poured another glass and handed that to him. I drank from the bottle. 'Here. Let's celebrate. I died today. Good news, and I'm celebrating.'

'Oh, Nicholas,' he said, sighing. He just held the glass. 'Mama told me to check on you. She was worried about you, said you could hardly get on the bus.'

'I'm fine,' I said.

He looked around. 'This is a nice place.'

'Your key is under the cookie jar in the kitchen.'

Papa went to the kitchen. I heard him move the cookie jar. He came back and sat down at my desk. No matter where I have lived, Papa sits down at my desk, sideways in the chair, sometimes leaning chin on fist on the back of the straight chair.

'I died today,' I said.

'I heard you say that.'

'You don't believe me?'

'No. You look a little pickled, but not dead.' He sat up straight. 'Something new,' he said knowingly.

'Goddamn you!' I suddenly realized that he was crawling around in me, snooping. 'Get out, get *out*!'

'I'm out,' he said, sipping his vodka. 'It wasn't very pleasant there anywhere, Kolya. But I couldn't help it. You're broadcasting full level. What's her name again?'

'W'hat's this "her"? You can't know that kind of shit, you're not telepathic. No form, no words, no names.' I wanted to fling something at him, but didn't. Couldn't.

'I recognize it without words. Nicholas, do you want me to get some help for you?'

I leaned back against the bookcase and just looked at him. He only said that when I frightened him, either to get at me, or because he really meant it. I sobered up a bit.

'A man asked my boss about me. The same man. His name is Miller.'

I nodded. 'He's been here, too. He's everywhere. Damn fucker's probably God. He's everywhere. Nothing I can do about it.'

'Kolya, maybe we should talk to him. Together. I don't think this is good for you.'

'You just want me safe and locked away again, don't you? You'll get me some day, won't you, Papa?'

'Nicholas,' he said, pained.

The lock clicked.

We stopped. Papa rose out of his chair. 'He has followed me!'

The door opened. First, Jack looked at me, then at my father.

'Come in,' I said, relieved. I didn't think that she would come over, after Friday afternoon, and had forgotten we'd arranged to be together.

'Hi,' she whispered. Shy? She closed the door behind her. 'Are you all right?'

'Just drunk,' I said, trying to stand.

She came into the center of the room, and glanced at my father. 'Hello,' she said softly.

My father, still standing, offered his hand. 'How do you do? I'm Alexander Dal, Kolya's father.' I noticed how stiff his English sounded, as if he hadn't been practicing it.

'I'm Jack,' she said, smiling, 'I thought you were the bogey man.'

Papa seemed to wince. He drank up, then snapped his

fingers under his chin. I poured him another. I understood suddenly that Jack was hurting him.

'See this lovely hair, Papa?' I said, pointing to Jack's head. 'It'll be all grey and even lovelier than this by the time she's forty.'

Jack just looked at us quietly.

'I had better go,' Papa said.

'She doesn't understand Russian,' I said to him, 'Was there something you wanted to tell me?'

'I just wanted to make sure you're all right. Do you want me to stay or will your friend take care of you?'

'I don't know,' I said, studying Jack, who was watching us speak with some interest. 'I think we have to fix something first.'

'She is hot.'

'I know,' I said. 'Isn't she sweet, though, Papa?'

'Be careful. I'm going to stay at the Holiday Inn off the turnpike if you need me. All right? I don't want to leave you, but I understand. Just call me there if you need me.'

'Come by before you leave tomorrow then. Please, Papa. I'm sorry I am so drunk.'

'I see that she's calming you down, even though she's hot. That's good.' He put down his glass. 'Forgive us, we are rude to you,' he said to Jack in English. 'I hope that we'll meet again.'

Jack nodded, smiling tightly. 'Nice to meet you . . . ' She hesitated.

'Alex,' he said. He backed away from her toward the door. 'Good night, Kolya.'

'Good night, Papa.'

In the silence that Papa left behind, Jack looked at me. 'Now I do understand why you have such an accent.'

I sat down in the rocking chair.

She stood uncertainly in the middle of the room, still wearing her jacket. 'I didn't know whether to come over or not.'

'Why?'

'I thought you might be busy.'

'Come over here to me.'

'No.' She sat on the floor about four feet from me. 'I had no right to be upset, but when I saw you with someone else, I felt awful. Jealousy is stupid – if you like someone else, well, that's the way it is. If you like me, too, I guess I'll have to see it that way. I just couldn't help . . . '

I couldn't say anything without making it worse.

'But what really bothers me is that you lied to me.'

'Lied?'

'About someone after you.'

'That has nothing to do with this. Did you think I made that up so that I could bring women here? We talked about that the day I moved in. I would only have to tell you. After all, this is my home.'

'But who is after you?' she asked miserably.

'I can't tell you.'

'Are you in trouble?'

I laughed. 'I was born in trouble.'

We couldn't look each other in the eye without glancing away. I wanted to tell her how awful it had been with Elaine, but it didn't even matter. That had been so long ago in my life, so unimportant. I could hardly remember. There was still too much hanging between us, though. I really wanted to tell her that I'd met her mother. That *was* important. But I had promised Susanne I would be silent about it.

'Jack,' I said, 'I wish I could tell you how much I care about you.'

She was unmoving, her shoulders hunched.

'Don't you feel a difference? Isn't it different from anything you've felt before?'

She nodded.

'I want to hold you,' I said.

'You're disgustingly drunk. It bothers me that you drink so much, Kolya. You're such a nice, gentle person, but . . . You probably couldn't even walk across the room without help.'

I didn't want to try. She crushed me with her observation. I sat in the chair. What was I going to do now? I thought I heard something at the back door and turned.

'What's the matter?' she asked.

I leaned back, realizing that I'd probably imagined it. Probably water dripping off the roof. 'Jack, I need your help.'

'Doing what?'

'Just help.' I held out my hand.

She stood and pulled me up out of the chair. 'Come on. I'll put you to bed.'

'No. I mean, I'm afraid . . . of dying alone.'

'What are you talking about?' she asked, annoyed.

I followed her to the bedroom. I lay on the bed, dizzy drunk, couldn't keep my eyes closed. 'I love you,' I said.

'Go to sleep.'

'I'm clearer now than when I'm sober. Really. The fog goes away and I can think. I love you.' I reached for her and interrupted her as she took her shoes off. 'Stay with me. Stay.'

I fell asleep with my arm around Jack's neck, afraid she would leave me alone.

When I woke early in the morning, it was still dark. Jack was having an uncomfortable dream. I nudged her a little, she stirred, and the dream changed. I had an awful head, my mouth was fuzzy and bitter. I needed to pee and wanted a cigarette, but was too sleepy to move right away. Watching Jack breathe, I was still for a long time. It was five-fifteen when I realized that I was so awake that to think of sleep was futile.

I was sober, too. Surprising, considering the amount of alcohol I had consumed.

Jack's dreams stirred again. I wanted to know them this time, because they are part of her. She is so strong, so good, so right, her dreams must be good, too. (I thought this as I snuggled against her.) Perhaps if I know her and understand how she works, I could learn to be strong and good and right, and she would love me. Maybe I could be different from what I am . . .

She came awake. I felt her disorientation until she opened her eyes. Couldn't see her face, but I knew when she remembered where she was. I pretended to sleep on, to feel her as if she were alone, without the reflection of my awareness in her.

I was exploring her most secret feelings when it all went sour. She started thinking about It. I wasn't prepared for that at all; I had expected a didactic moment of enlightenment. It was a great slap inside my head. I jerked, I think, but Jack was only vaguely aware of me.

She was *concentrating* on Death. Trying to eye it down.

I didn't even think of the fever; everything went numb except for a sensation of pressure. Her emotional thumbs pressed my eyes. I heard a crackling, somewhere far back in my skull, snap, snap, snap, as my grey cells fired.

Jack sat up. 'Jesus,' she said.

I was afraid of seizure. 'Bring me vodka, please.'

'Kolya, I don't think you should. You're burning up.'

I got out of bed, somehow, and headed for the kitchen.

It was worse. I was making it worse because now Jack followed, thinking that I might die. The tremors made it hard for me to walk.

What are you doing, Jack asked me, but the boom-boom-crackle buried her voice. I smelled the antiseptic of the boys' hall. They were putting their icy hands on me again.

What's the matter with you, crazy?

What's the matter with you, crazy?

Are you crazy?

Crazy?

I think I may have screamed, but then it may have been Jack. She put the bottle in my hands, helped me hold it to my mouth.

The static continued for some time, but I remember clearing up, naked, damp, sitting on the cold tiles of the kitchen floor with the bright light on. We both panted, and that rasping sound echoed back at us.

'DTs?' she asked.

I shook my head. I felt another presence, but nothing

substantial. Who was that? 'Is someone here?' I asked.

'No.' She looked around.

I got up. Still shaking. Muscles felt as if I'd been carrying a couple of tons for a mile. I went to bed and slept.

The fire in my head. The fire in my head.

I woke saying that. Jack wasn't in the room, but she was in the house. I guessed that she was in the kitchen, soon her feet pattered in the hallway. She looked in.

We stared at each other, embarrassed.

'Coffee?'

'Yes, please,' I said. I dressed, stiffly.

We sat at the kitchen table silently for a while. Jack read the morning paper, which she had apparently gone out for while I slept. A box of chocolate doughnuts sat on the table, but I couldn't eat. I drank my coffee.

I thought about calling my father, but he is always so worried about me, I wasn't sure. He worries without reason, I suppose. He had tried most of the time to make things easier for me, but they were things that couldn't be anything but difficult. I remember the first time he told me that I would have to visit the psychiatrist.

I had been so afraid, but he hugged me. 'Don't tell him anything about it – don't tell him that other people affect you.'

I thought I had understood, but I hadn't.

'Tell him that you've been upset because your mother and father have been fighting, and now you feel badly because your mother left and made your father sad. Then he won't bother you about anything else.'

'That's true, Papa, I *am* sad.'

Papa hugged me tighter.

In a moment, he said, 'But, don't tell him everything like that. Let him ask you. Pretend that it bothers you to talk about it. Then when he hears you say these things, he will think that he's found a treasure. Do you understand?'

I remember trying to sense what my father was feeling then. That was my first experience of loneliness – Papa routinely shut himself off from me, put a little vodka in my glass every night, even though Grandmama told him not to any more because of what the school nurse had said. He was sorrowing for Miranda, my mother, and didn't want to share it with me.

And there, Miranda had the last blow after all. I discovered Alexander Fyodorovich has walls. Not hard, impenetrable walls, I know now, but a persistent and resistant barrier that he can use against me. I've never discovered my walls, but my father is the only one left who would recognize them anyway. I've built my walls from words and actions, out of anger. I've made him suffer so that I could pretend I had my isolation. I've punished him for many things.

'Some day, Kolya,' he said, 'when you have a wife, and a son, you'll understand. You'll see how good and bad life is. I loved your mother, but she wasn't right for us. I should have told her everything, but she never would have understood. Not Miranda.'

And I knew that if I was ever to have a wife, I would have to tell her everything first.

Thinking of this, I looked at Jack. So quiet today, Jack was. She leaned against the kitchen wall and picked at her doughnut. Perhaps she was afraid of or for me. I didn't know which because I was numb.

'I need to apologize,' I said.

She shrugged. 'Not really. It's your business, your liver. Just makes me sad to see you waste yourself like that. You really don't know how frustrating it is to see you destroy yourself, but I guess eventually something will happen to make you realize what you're doing.'

'I know what it sounds like to say this, but you don't quite understand everything.'

She looked at me. 'I suppose you have a *reason* to drink.'

'In a way.' I took a deep breath. 'What happened this morning . . . It's part of an illness. Alcohol helps. It isn't the cause.'

She was still. Then she tapped her fingernails on the table. 'Illness?'

'Yes. I have a . . . syndrome,' I said, finally finding that damned word in my memory.

'Oh, that,' she said, 'you mentioned it once.' But she sounded skeptical.

'I was drunk last night and I apologize for that. I didn't think you would come over.'

'Well, I thought I had been assuming too much, but I decided that we should talk about it.' She glanced at me. She was asking me what had happened.

'Right at this time, you're the only woman I care about.'

We were quiet again for a short while. I felt better and started to eat a doughnut.

'Kolya, I have some news. I've gotten a wonderful job for the summer. For now, in fact, part-time. It's incredible luck.'

'What's that?'

'I was in my anthro class and my professor asked me to stop by after class. He said that he'd been asked to recommend behavioral science students for a job with a visiting professor. Me! I can't believe it. I'm a good student, but I never get into all that extra junk that gets students noticed, you know? So I went over and talked to Dr Miller – '

'Miller?'

'Know him?'

'Oh, no, I don't think so,' I said coolly. Miller! That was the name Papa said last night.

'All I have to do is some typing, interviewing, a little research, some statistics. If only he knew how I had struggled to get that B in stat!' She laughed.

'What's he like? A nice boss?'

'Oh, yeah, he seems very nice. He looked a little familiar, but I can't think where I've seen him. He's from back east, somewhere, not New York, though. He's doing some research on drugs. Usual stuff. He said he was going to be teaching a class the first summer session.'

I was trying to hold on as she told me this. I couldn't believe it was happening. Here is the one woman that I really love and there is the one man determined to tear me apart and *she* will lead *him* to me.

Somehow I managed to stay conversational. 'I thought only psychiatrists had anything to do with drugs, he must be a psychiatrist.'

'Well, he's just studying them, not dispensing them.'

I just nodded. Perhaps it's not the same man. Who am I kidding? I know it is going to happen eventually. Something really exciting has set him on this path – glory, personal vindication of some kind . . . But why would a man really go to all this trouble? He will not stop until he's bagged me, but I won't tell him anything. To move halfway across the country, twist the arm of the university, and then hire my girlfriend, he is determined. I will have to be very cautious. I will have to talk to him, but I need to prepare myself somehow. I simply won't talk. I just won't say what he wants to hear. No one can force me to say what I don't want to say.

'I suppose this is a one-in-a-million job. Something you can't pass up,' I said.

Jack laughed again. She was so happy! 'It's great. It's made for an impractical person like me who knows how to do things no one else needs to know.'

'Well, I'm glad you don't have to be a waitress this summer. I hate kissing women that smell like pizza all the time.'

We talked at the table for another few hours, drinking coffee, slowly devouring the doughnuts, feeling the freedom of the weekend. She invited me to her house for dinner next weekend. I said yes against my better judgment, but I want to see Susanne again. I feel constrained, not talking to Jack about her mother, but maybe meeting her officially will take care of that.

My muscles were sore and stiff. I decided to work that off by sweeping out the carport and doing a little yardwork that I'd promised the landlord. Jack sat on the back step, reading, as I swept and hosed.

Papa came by and we all went out for pizza (Jack had

grown hungry for it because I'd mentioned it earlier). I thought my father was rather charming and funny to Jack; we spoke English the whole time, except for haggling over the check. He asserted his authority over me and said it was a contribution to my education.

We came back. While Jack was in the bathroom, I told him about Miller and Jack's job.

'I can't get away from it.'

'You'll be all right,' Papa said.

But we were both worried. It was the same worry between us. But Papa changed the subject and said he was glad that I have Jack. He knows that I care for her. He said he had to leave, that he was going to spend the rest of the weekend visiting Grandmama.

After Papa left, Jack said she had to go home, too. I sit here alone now, and I am thinking about how quickly I can pack up everything I would take with me and go away. But where would I go?

5 April

Jack told me that she finally talked to her mother. Julie had gone. Her father was mowing the lawn, and Jack had just been sitting at the kitchen table working on her term paper. Susanne came and sat with her. They talked about her class for a moment, then Jack said Susanne asked her where she had been all night on Saturday. She told her that she'd spent the night with me. As Jack was telling me this, she seemed to have experienced a great relief. So many things were swept away by five minutes' conversation with her mother.

Susanne told Jack that she would have been upset about Jack spending the night with a man she didn't know (so Susanne wasn't going to tell, either) without Jack phoning, but things had changed, her attitudes had changed.

'We were really talking around it,' Jack said. Her mother

said that she had not slept all that night, but she was thinking that it was okay, that Jack was old enough to make decisions like that. In fact, she envied her for being able to take advantage of opportunities.

Then Susanne asked Jack if she was going to miss her when she was dead.

'It was like lightning had struck me to hear her say that,' Jack told me. 'I started crying, and she started crying, and we talked about how much we love each other, and like each other. I told her how sick it makes me to think of her dying.'

They even laughed because they both had to go and wash their faces and look fresh or the husband/father would find them conspiring about death and dying together.

How strange, how strange.

6 April

I think I'm in love.

I can't believe it. Me. Nicholas Alexandrovich in love. She cares a lot about me, too, though I don't know what she calls it.

God, it's miserable. It was easy to exist when I was alone, just to wake up every morning and do what I had to do. Never gave a second thought to when I would see her, how long we could be together, what she was doing when she wasn't in sight . . . But now, I think of these things. And Jack makes me linger in bed – lying there with my eyes shut pretending she's there if she's not, and when she is, just holding her.

I wonder what she would think if she knew that I ravish her every care and delight with a certain knowledge of what her feelings are. She can't hide from me.

Oh, but when she makes me sick . . . frightening. I don't know how I let it happen. I don't know what I can do about it, either. Wait. It'll be over some day, and that will be a relief and a sadness to me. I think of Susanne and already I'm mournful, but she still lives.

I have control. I really do. Mikhail was mad, but I'm sane.

Dr Benjamin Miller is a clever bastard. I knew that he would trace me through Jack as soon as he saw us that day, but he's doing it so well. If he'd just taken her for coffee it would have been one thing, but he's given her an opportunity that an undergraduate can't resist. Took it completely out of my hands. I couldn't beg her not to take that job. And now, well, I'm entangled . . .

Miller won't get me. I just won't say anything. The only person that can get me is another psychic, and that person would be as deserving of a lobotomy as myself.

I can handle it. Especially with this new strength. I know this strength – it comes from Jack.

She spent last night with me. Told her parents, too. ('When are we going to meet this guy?') Ate dinner here. I made cornbread and fried chicken. Then we decided to do some homework. I had to type up a paper. My desk was a mess, so I moved the typewriter into the kitchen; Jack remained in the living room.

I felt Miller come to the house.

Unmistakable. At first, I was just startled. How did he find my house again? But it isn't surprising, since he seems to gain everyone's co-operation wherever he goes. Or probably followed one of us when we weren't being careful. Jack seems to think it is a game I've invented, and isn't very cautious. Who knows, she's so trusting and honest that she may have given him my address if he asked her the right way.

I stopped typing and the house was quiet. I wondered if he would come to the door. He seemed to be waiting in his car, or perhaps he was on foot, just walking by. I recognized him – he's a distinctive combination of emotions.

Papa is better at locating people by their aura than I am. He can pinpoint, narrow down his readings in a crowd and probe a perfect stranger, know exactly who it is, and shut everyone else out, like fine focus. We used to play hide and seek in the grocery store now and then. I'd be over by the bread, he'd be at the meat, and would come and peek around and grin at me. But I could never find him if there were people between us, though I knew he was *somewhere*.

I felt Miller come up closer to the house, but he was hesitant. I felt him getting close to the kitchen window. It made me so uneasy to have him slowly moving toward me that I got up and went into the living room and pretended to be looking for something in the desk drawers. I didn't want Jack to know that I knew the doorbell was going to ring in just a moment. I was trying to think of what to say, how to say it, wondering what he was going to ask me. What could he say with Jack there? She didn't even look at me. She was lost in bones and pottery in her textbook.

I got the shakes. I was cold, waiting for him to do something. But he just stood outside.

He seemed to be hesitant because it wasn't safe, because he didn't think I was alone. The man is so lucid I can almost read his thoughts. But he's not cold, not intellect without the human freight. I would like him if he didn't hunt me. Maybe he would like me. We may have been friends in another situation.

He started moving around the house. I felt him going around to the side, then across the front again, and up into the carport. I was nearly ready to vomit. By delaying (maybe he meant to do that), he was making me more and more anxious. I was beginning to feel that if he came to the door I would have a heart attack, or stroke, or an asthma attack.

I wanted to fling the front door open and say, 'Will you stop wandering about and come in?' But that would be telling on myself.

Jack looked up at me from her book. She watched me. 'Why aren't you typing?' Earlier, I'd told her to keep her hot hands off me until I'd finished, that I wasn't going to move until the report was typed.

I couldn't think of anything. I'd forgotten that she

couldn't know what was happening. I was thinking that Jack was letting it roll off in her usual rational way because she was unafraid of Miller.

I made a stupid noise, like, 'Uhhhh . . . '

She smiled at me.

And then I wasn't afraid. Suddenly it didn't matter because she loves me, and she would help me. I will tell her everything some day and she'll understand.

I went back to the kitchen to type again.

Miller never knocked. He got back into his car (I heard a car door shut quietly) and went away.

I wish I could tell her all tomorrow. But not yet, not yet.

14 April

When I stood at the front door of the Berdos' house, I tried to brace myself. If I knew then what I know now, I wouldn't have gone in. I had been drinking most of the afternoon, just a little, but frequently. I wasn't sure how I would survive the evening with the family. I brought my flask, tucked into my jacket, because I wasn't even sure if they drank at all. I would have to have something. How little I knew about them! Were they religious? Were they friendly or cold, ordinary, strange? What would they think of this man who is bedding their daughter regularly? Were we going to play pachisi for hours or watch television or talk about the rise of the American labor union?

I had to remind myself that I already knew half the family. Julie, the kid sister, I didn't worry about. It was the Awful Father that Jack so fears. He would be sizing me up, thinking me too old and seedy for his freshly-scrubbed daughter. He would smell alcohol on my breath, I would seem foreign, unsuccessful . . . Why would a *man* aspire to become a librarian, handing out gothic novels all day?

If you want Jack, you have to do this, I told myself. And I rang the bell.

Jack opened the door immediately. She kissed me, then said, 'Oh, Kolya, you've been drinking already!' Distressed.

'Not drunk though,' I said, glad that she hadn't said it any louder. We were alone in the living room. I looked around. The house was a little warm, probably from the oven, and smelled of bread, vegetables, and coffee. Somewhere a hint of charcoal and lighter fluid. The house was furnished in muted colors – tan, beige, light brown – very ordinary and comfortable, a bit on the expensive side with a broad banistered stairway, huge living room, a bookcase topped with leafy plants, and an oak dining room set.

Susanne came out of the kitchen. It took my breath away to see her so suddenly; we looked at each other with this secret between us. A lot of hair had fallen out since I'd seen her, she was thinner and a touch more golden, but seemed perfectly cheerful as Jack introduced us. 'Glad to meet you,' she said. I know I shouldn't have, it was silly, but instead of shaking her hand, I kissed it. I felt it would tell her something that I wanted to say.

Susanne laughed. 'Charming,' she said.

Jack shook her head. She seemed to think I was pouring it on because I was drunk.

The Awful Father and Little Julie came in together from the back door, through the kitchen. Jack introduced me to her father, Paul, and he thrust his hand out at me. Somehow, he wasn't what I had expected, but then I don't think I quite met his image, either. We shook hands firmly. He was a little less than medium height, energetic, sandy-haired, muscular. Everything I'm not. Seemed friendly enough.

And Julie. She stared at me without inhibition. She was unlike any of the others, taller and giving an impression of being willowy, with long hair the color of her father's and big eyes. 'Hi,' she said, standing behind Jack.

'We've got steaks ready to grill. You're not a vegetarian, are you?' Paul asked.

'Oh, no, quite omnivorous.'

'What? Oh, well, would you like a drink then?' He rubbed his palms on his corduroy trousers, searching around the room, turning toward the kitchen.

'Sure,' I said, knowing Jack wouldn't like that. I wanted Paul to relax. It must be hard for a man to have his daughter adore another man completely unlike himself, and not understand the words he used, either.

'Scotch? Wine? Jack Daniels?'

'I'll have some wine.'

'I'll get it,' Susanne said.

''Sall right, Suz, why don't you sit down. I'll get it,' Paul insisted.

Susanne sat down abruptly at the dining room table and glared at Paul.

I was glad that I'd already had a few before I walked in. I looked down at Susanne. 'May I see the back yard?' I asked, because I needed to cool off.

'Yes, let's go out there. It's a nice evening.' She seemed as anxious as I was to get out.

We all marched out the back door. Jack disappeared into the garage and returned with an armload of webbed lawn chairs. I helped her unfold them, and we formed a semi-circle around the portable grill. I felt as if I were in a magazine ad, not in someone's home. I got to sit between Jack and Susanne, which was exactly what I would have arranged, had someone asked. Jack brushed my hand with her fingers and gave me a smile to let me know that everything was all right so far.

Paul brought Jack and me a glass of wine, then went back inside the house.

'Jack says your father came from Russia,' Susanne said.

'Yes. When he was a small boy.'

Susanne and I leaned back in our chairs; there was something lazily familiar about the way we looked at each other across the few feet of space between chairs. She sipped a glass of water. 'I used to work at the university, a few years ago, in the admissions office. I think I remember you. I remember trying to place your accent.'

'I thought you looked familiar, too,' I said, feeling the good nature of this game. We are friends already.

'I got pretty good at accents,' she said. 'Lots of foreign students have problems with their records, but of course, you aren't foreign, are you?'

'No.'

'You speak Russian?' It was the first thing Julie had said since her shy hello.

'Yes.' This always fascinates people. Why? I doubt that any Hispanic is questioned so closely about his parents speaking Spanish at home. 'My grandmother never has gotten much past saying hello and shopping in *angliski*. My father does better. I do best of all, don't you think?' I looked at Jack. She nodded.

'But you speak Russian in your sleep.'

Susanne looked startled, but then she laughed. Julie's eyes widened. Paul came from the kitchen with a platter of raw steak.

'How do you like your steak?' he asked me.

'Medium.'

'I took Russian,' Julie said, 'when I was in the eleventh grade. I don't remember much. Uh . . . *ya ne zniyou*,' she said, and blushed.

I nodded. 'That will keep you out of trouble,' I said. I wondered how old Julie is. Still in high school? Out a year? In college, too? Jack never separated Julie from the family when talking about her.

'What does that mean? Susanne asked.

'I don't know,' Julie replied.

Jack and Susanne laughed at her, even Paul glanced over with a grin. Julie turned even redder.

'It means "I don't know," ' she said indignantly.

I asked her in Russian, 'Why are you so shy, pretty girl?'

She smiled. 'I understood part of that,' and I knew which part as she began self-consciously to toy with the ends of her hair.

'What? What?' Jack asked.

I told Jack what I'd said and she laughed, punching her

111

sister's arm playfully. 'She's being coy. She's a regular hell-raiser but she gets away with it because of that sweet face.'

'I am not. How would *you* know anyway?' Julie said.

'I know.' Jack sounded like an older sister.

'What does your father do?' Paul asked in the midst of a greasy sizzle.

'He works in a bakery.'

'I admire you for putting yourself through college like this,' Paul said.

He seemed to have some misapprehension about how hard-working I am, but I didn't set him straight. 'I haven't made it yet,' I said, but immediately realized that that wasn't the right approach, either. I took a sip of wine. Jack looked at me uneasily. The interrogation was on.

'I never got to college,' Paul said. 'But it was easier when I was a kid to get a decent job right out of high school. When Suz and I first got married, I worked construction, then got into real estate. Not a bad living at all.' Paul drank from his Scotch.

Again, it seemed to me that I could have written the script for this family. It made me uncomfortable to see through them, to understand them without knowing them. There were no mysteries to Paul.

Susanne slapped her arm. 'Damned bugs.'

'Well, I'm sure your folks being immigrants, you can appreciate hard times. Your family was poor, wasn't it?'

I shook my head. 'No, not really. We had a big farm back ho – back there, and they brought some money with them.'

Paul flipped the steak with ease. A timer buzzed in the kitchen. Jack squeezed my hand and got up to tend whatever it signaled.

'We're going to eat inside, aren't we?' Susanne asked, waving her hand at another grey speck of insect.

'Sure, Suz, if you like.' His voice was hollow.

Susanne got out of the lawn chair, and slammed the screen door as she went inside. Julie looked around as if wondering how she managed to be left behind. 'Guess I'll go and see about the table,' she said, and was gone.

Paul poked at the steaks busily. I was getting hungry from the smell of the meat, but also getting tense. What was going on here? Was I supposed to be interviewed by the head of the household for being Jack's friend?

'Jack doesn't bring her boyfriends here,' Paul said. 'Only once before. Guess she thinks we'll scare them off,' he laughed.

I smiled as naturally as I could. Since the women had gone, I had been sitting on the edge of the lawn chair, but finally decided to stand by the grill with him. We were destined to have a conversation of sorts. 'I never have done this myself,' I said.

Paul looked up at me. 'You serious? Used to be that parents met their kids' dates all the time. Now . . . So you like Jack a lot, I guess.'

I nodded. 'Yes.'

'You love her?' he asked after a pause.

'Maybe I do. We haven't known each other long.'

He sighed. 'You know . . . our situation.'

'You mean Susanne's illness?'

He nodded. It took him a long time to gather himself after speaking so far. I could see the struggle in him. I moved back a step, afraid, knowing that he could sear me straight through the alcohol.

I am good at reading faces; I've always matched what's inside with what's outside, something Papa said he never did. He was lazy. But I recognize lip twitches, eye movements, sighs for what they represent in the soul.

Paul grieves. Susanne is right; she is just about dead as far as he is concerned. He's relinquished her presence and now it does nothing to soothe him, only stirs his wounds painfully.

Thank God I was full of alcohol. I didn't want to experience the pain that I saw.

'I loved Susanne,' he said.

I was surprised to hear him talk. 'I remember . . . ' He chuckled. Smoke smarted his eyes and he waved at the

113

plumes rising out of the grill. 'I hadn't known Susanne very long, either, maybe a couple of months, when I decided that she was for me. She was the prettiest girl around.'

'Still is,' I said.

'And I've never been sorry.' He blinked.

'That's a good and rare thing.'

We stood there a few moments. How had I come into this situation? The whole family is drawn to tell me everything. Oh, I know I have a sympathetic face. How could I not when I am a mirror? All my life people had seen in me the listener for their troubles, no matter what, no matter when, no matter how. I have only been able to avoid clinging friendships by being rude and elusive. But this is definitely the strangest entire situation. I, a stranger (always a stranger), take turns with them all to hear their grief. A sin-eater.

'Look, I know I may be talking a fast pitch here,' Paul said, 'but Jack's a good kid. She looks so reckless to me, but she's not stupid. She does things *I* wouldn't have done at her age, but she's got a good head. I wasn't as smart, and I'm kinda proud of her. If she should leave . . . for instance, to get married, she'll still be my kid, and I'll pay for her education.'

I didn't know what to say. I've never had a father try to give his daughter to me before.

'I guess Julie's more like me,' he said. 'She can never make a decision without six opinions and a few threats.'

'I think you have a lovely family.'

We stood, concentrating on the steaks. Paul drank; I drank. We talked about how done the steaks might be, and how the fire might be a little cool. Paul has great expertise in outdoor grills.

'I kind of expected someone different, you know?' Paul said, looking right at me. 'Maybe someone younger, like the other students. I like hard-working guys like you, doing things the tough way.'

How uncomfortable I was! If only you knew, Paul, what would you say? There is a monster roaming your land, bedding your daughter, and you stand chatting with him so paternally. If he knew he would be reeling her back in a second. But, then, what if Jack knew . . . ? I had doubts suddenly. Everything is so *ordinary* at the Berdos', except for a silver-haired woman who is slowly turning orange and dying.

I must listen. I must take all that they offer for its value, nod my head. I understand, I understand what you are saying. And yet, I feel so lonely standing in the midst of people, knowing all of them so well that their feelings are my own. I cannot really be a part of them. And I cannot speak.

I looked up at the sky. The bellies of the clouds were turning pink. The top of the sky is so far, far away. And beyond that, stars and galaxies and maybe other universes. All I could think about was the hope I had that Jack would come home with me because I felt so lonely being with people.

'Guess that's it,' Paul said, loading the steaks back onto the platter.

At dinner, Susanne hardly spoke or ate. She stared at things on the table. We talked a little about a big bombing in the Middle East that had occurred that day, about the food, about musical instruments that we'd played in our childhoods. Everyone had tried once and given up. I had played the clarinet in elementary school – until I was taken out of school.

Afterwards, Julie rushed upstairs to dress for a date. We settled into the living room, me on the sofa beside Jack, Paul in a recliner, and Susanne oddly apart in a straight-backed chair she'd pulled in from the dining room.

'So, did the Communists change things a lot for your family?' Paul asked, picking up a thread of conversation from earlier. I guessed that they, too, had seen *Doctor Zhivago*.

'Not as much as for other people, other places. My grandfather heard that there were a lot of changes after they came here. The revolution was still young.'

'Did your whole family come over?'

'Everyone that was left,' I said, feeling under pressure.

'So you must have a lot of relatives here.'

'No.' My voice went faint. 'Only my grandparents and my father made it to America.' I could feel Jack's eyes on me, wondering. Here was a piece of mystery, and she was thinking about that.

We talked about families for a long time. Paul's family had always figured that their family was French, perhaps from Bordeaux, and the name had been Anglicized over generations. But it was possible that they were Swiss. Susanne had been born Riley, but all she knew was that somewhere back in her ancestry there had been Indians - probably Cherokee. That's where the dark eyes are from, I'll wager.

It struck me how strange a country this is; people may have cousins in so many lands, never knowing it. Does the family in France have any idea of the kinship to a real estate agent in Colorado?

I know everything about my family. And I know that there are no relatives left other than the three of us. Anyone related to the Dals had been taken into our family; even sons-in-law had gone against custom and come to live with the Dals so that the sons of that union could be 'with their own kind.' The Dals had married little, except for that last generation. Old Nicholas had been an appealing man and the village had taken to the family somewhat, which is why the house had been bursting at the seams with family at the end.

Of course, I said as little as I could about the family. I listened. I watched. I rather liked Paul Berdo in a way, or at least, I was feeling sympathy for him. He was struggling to stay afloat in a situation that called for sinking. He was paradoxically buoyed up and weighed down by the presence of Susanne. He hardly looked at her, but watched all around her to make sure everything was all right.

Jack kept an eye on me to see that I didn't get drunk. Julie ran up and down the stairs, checking to see if her date had arrived yet. She was taking elaborate care to appear prettily casual.

And Susanne . . . Would I be so fascinated if she weren't dying? I think so. She has a quality in her presence that draws me. Jack has some of it, and now I see the source. I think that Jack will gain more of this integrity as she matures. Jack will be a good sort of grown woman. But she'll never have that . . . that soulfulness . . . that I see in Susanne.

We had a pleasant evening up to a point. Then, Susanne leaned toward me, holding out her slender arm. 'May I have a sip of your wine?' she asked me.

I felt Jack's fingers dig into my thigh. And at the same time, Paul rose out of her chair. 'Suz, I'll get you . . . '

But I handed her my wine glass. She looked at Paul. 'It's not catching, dear,' she said, and took a delicate drink.

I noticed then, when Susanne handed me the glass again, that she looked a little ill. A strange color surrounded her eyes and mouth. She'd hardly eaten, and the wine was the first thing she'd had to drink.

Paul sat back, a floundering motion in his hands. 'Have you traveled much, Kolya?' he said suddenly.

'No . . . ' I began, but didn't know what to say. The room was a flurry though we all sat still.

'He doesn't even have a car,' Jack said. 'Mom, would you like me to fix you some tea?'

Susanne turned her head slowly and looked at her daughter. Now, I understand what Jack meant about that look – dark and icy, a challenge of sorts. 'No, I would like a glass of wine.'

Jack got up from the sofa. 'Here, Kolya, I'll refill yours, too.' She reached for my glass though it was half-full.

I drank the rest of my wine before handing it over. When I saw Susanne's face, it was changed. The iciness was gone. I am unafraid of the touch of her lips on my glass.

Jack said, 'I'll bring the bottle.' She returned with the wine and two more glasses. She poured for us all, except Paul, who still had Scotch.

117

The phone rang. Jack answered it in the dining room; it seemed to be for her. I jealously wondered who called her. Paul glanced at Susanne, but she was drinking down the wine, half of it at one gulp. I drank, too, seeing that things were getting awful.

Julie ran down the stairs one more time. ' 'Bye!' she called, and sprinted out the front door, looking very teenage and long-legged.

Jack hung up and came back, a half-smile on her face. 'That was . . . '

Susanne jumped from her chair and ran up the stairs as quickly as Julie had come down. From the top of the stairs came a gurgling, retching sound, then coughing. I felt sick from the sound of it. Jack ran up the stairs after her mother.

Paul leaned back in his chair, hollow and drained.

'Mother, let me in!' Jack said, pounding at the door.

I stood. I could no longer sit, but didn't know what to do.

Susanne vomited more. Fiercely. Jack pounded and shouted at her mother to let her in.

Paul covered his face with one hand.

'Would you like me to call a doctor?' I asked, desperate to do something.

Paul shook his head, his face still hidden. He made a strange sucking sigh.

I sat again, waiting. I drank the rest of my wine and poured more. 'Can I get you anything?' I asked Paul, then realized that he was sobbing.

He shook his head. Then he sat upright and wiped his face with his meaty hands. 'No. Sorry. I just can't believe that Susanne . . . '

'But she's not gone yet,' I said. It sounded awful and out of place for me to say anything at all, so I decided to shut up and wait until Jack came down, then I would go. I was sweating. I was feeling dangerously affected.

Paul went into the kitchen. I heard him get ice out of the refrigerator. Jack came down and stood on the stairway. 'Where's Dad?' she asked.

I pointed to the kitchen.

They met in the dining room. 'I guess she's all right, but she won't let me in.' She started to move close to her father, perhaps to hug him.

'Leave me alone!' he shouted, and turned toward the back door. The screen slammed behind him.

Jack started after him. I called to her. 'I'm leaving.'

'Oh . . . ' She frowned. 'Wait a minute.' And she was after her father.

'Hell,' I said, refilling my wine glass. I wanted to go to the mountains. Immediately. I wanted to take the bicycle and a pack and stay out there for a few days, sitting on a rock in the bright sun, just looking at brown grass, pines, and old rocks. I felt congestion in my mind. I was hot. The booze wasn't doing it. My knees and elbows were weakening. I had to get out. I had almost decided just to go and not wait for Jack to have her heart-to-heart with her father when the doorbell rang.

I sat, looking around me for help. 'Hell,' I said, and went to the door. I looked for a light switch to the porch. Guess who? I was staring right into the face of Dr Benjamin Miller.

'Is Jack here?' he asked.

'This may be a bad time.' I hoped I didn't sound too hoarse. 'Family problems.'

'But I called,' he said. 'May I come in?'

I opened the door. It wasn't my place to leave him standing there. He stepped in, scanning the room a little nervously. He wore a suit coat and loosened tie, and carried a manila envelope in one hand. I felt a twinge of something, seeing that he was so handsome and young-looking, thinking about Jack working closely with him. He looked up at me, as I am much taller, but he didn't betray any sign of recognition.

He held out his hand. 'Ben Miller.'

'Nicholas,' I said, hoping that my hand wasn't clammy. In fact, Miller's hand felt cold to mine.

'Pleased to meet you.'

'Do you want to leave a message?' I said. 'There's a

family emergency.' Susanne was doing her part to make it seem convincing with a constant retching cough.

'I see.' he studied me. 'Sorry I interrupted . . .'

I was sorry, too. How did he find out that I would be here tonight? Prying son of a bitch. He's been watching my house. Or watching this one? Take a good look at me, I thought. I was calming down. I endured it, him standing there, looking me over. What did he expect? Yellow eyes? Fangs and claws? No one will ever know about me. I'm freakish inside where you can't get to me. Smile, I told myself, smile.

I smiled.

'Well, if you could give her this.' He handed me the envelope. 'She can call me if she has any questions, all right?'

'She'll get it.'

'Thank you.' He glanced around to go out the door. But he gave me a last glance. The look shot right into me – a sort of curiosity and pleading. Maybe he thought he was going to break me down with emotional begging.

No way. Didn't touch me. I was too drunk, even if he could reach me.

' 'Bye,' I said.

' 'Bye,' he said.

I waited until I heard his car drive away, then I left the envelope on the coffee table and went home.

17 April

I'm in a nightmare. But there's so much good in it that I can't leave.

After I left the Berdos' on Saturday night I went up the road to my place by the creek, to my nest under the rock. That's where I belong when things are bad – under a rock. But I can lie there and there are no voices, no ticking of mechanical devices, only a buzzing insect now and then.

I have my own dreams here, my own feelings, not those of passersby. This is the spot where Nicholas Alexandrovich comes uncrumpled, like a piece of paper unwadding, as there is no one to crush me here.

I know this: I am in love with Jack. I've never felt this way before, but I want her. I don't know what I'll do if she'll have me – the thought of her getting to know me frightens me. She is an angel from the light side, what will she think of me when she knows all? I want her to want me. I think about her all the time now, and whenever I do or think something, somehow she's there.

This was the purest thing that I felt coming from me as I sat alone through that night.

And I know this, too: I can't run from Miller.

I'm going to have to tell her. But not yet. I am making up the words in my mind already. Papa's mistake has taught me that we can't take people into our family without telling them. This will be something I'll do gently, in small bits. I think she might love me, too.

But the cheerful attitude I had about getting through these troubles, the optimism generated by a night of peace, has been dampened by what's happened since that night.

I saw a strange thing. I was on that hill overlooking the town. The college is a patch of green trees, lawns, old ruddy buildings in the center of town. The business district forms a crescent around the university, and the old residential districts fan outward, gradually blending into the newer, the subdivisions and shopping malls. And all that comes to the edge of the dusty foothills, which rise into the edge of the Rocky Mountains. I like this view and always stop here. I like this town – it's small and yet there are bookstores, a variety of places to eat, things to see. But with only an hour's hard pedaling, I can be with the rabbits, mice, hawks, meadowlarks and beetles in one direction, or the pine and aspen of the mountains in another.

I saw fire in the town.

No – *on* the town. The whole thing. At first I thought it might be the sun rising, reflecting in the windows, but the sun was rising in my face as I came down the hills. I stopped, and said, 'No,' to myself, disbelieving the conflagration. But then I realized that it wasn't a real fire. Nothing was being consumed, nothing charred or even smoking. The town was covered with my own flames.

I sat down on the dry grass and watched until the flames went away, then bicycled home.

The first thing I saw when I opened the door was Susanne, rocking back and forth slowly in the rocking chair. Chalk-pale, dark circles under her eyes, wearing the same loose-fitting dress that she'd worn at dinner the night before. She barely lifted her head enough to look at me.

I thought she was a ghost. Susanne's dead and her ghost has come to say goodbye.

'Jack's gone to a phone,' she said, as if that explained everything I might want to know about her sitting in my house.

I was afraid. I hadn't a drop of alcohol in me and didn't know how she was going to affect me. As she rocked in the chair, the muscle of one calf tensed and relaxed, and tensed again. I watched her rather than move toward my bottle in the kitchen. Finally, I sat down at my desk, across the room from her. 'Are you all right?'

She smiled. 'Sure.' She turned her head a little to look more directly at me. 'I came here with Jack to get away. Hope you don't mind the intrusion.'

I felt so little coming from her. Her feelings were all a whisper. I leaned forward, and felt a little dizzy. I had the same sensation that one has in total darkness, that of holding up one's hand and not seeing it, or stepping onto unseen ground. But I could still hear her, smell, taste the world with clarity. We waited, in this still darkness.

Is she real, I wondered? I doubted myself, remembering the flames I'd seen earlier. Perhaps Susanne is made of the same stuff. I walked to her and put my hand on her head. I touched the wispy silvery hair, then felt the warmth of her face.

She is real.

When I touched her, she came alive. She looked up at me and I knew it all suddenly.

I sat down at her feet and she stopped rocking. I couldn't look away from her. How to describe it? It was being pulled to the center of things, resignation. Easy and peaceful, but exciting. It was like falling in love, but something deeper and stronger, larger than something as personal as love.

I was weakened by what she gave me.

Susanne put her hand on my shoulder. 'You understand, don't you?' she said. 'How do you do that?'

'I have the *pozhar-golava*,' I said, and it was the first time in my life I'd said the words to an American, to anyone. In truth, it was the first time I'd heard them in years. They sounded strange to me, but Susanne could have asked more and I would have told her everything. I was helpless before her.

She nodded, as if she knew what I'd said – I think she did somehow.

'Jack's gone to call a doctor,' she said softly. 'But I'm not going anywhere.' She took her hand from my shoulder and folded both hands in her lap, closing her eyes. 'I want to be with you when I die. I like you. You understand. You look at me when I make faces. You hear me say the things that they ignore.' She laughed (a whisper of a laugh, her voice was low) and said, 'Did you see Paul's face when you gave me your wine glass?'

I couldn't move. I wanted her to touch me again. But she *was* touching me. She was closer than any human has ever been. She drew me along with her someplace, and she had no idea that I was right alongside her.

She got up suddenly and walked into the bathroom. She left the door open and I could see her crouch at the toilet, heave out a bright red gush. There was blood everywhere, spattered on the floor, on the toilet, on Susanne's dress. Get rid of it, vomit the heart out. Such a long journey. Tired, tired, tired. She heaved again.

I must have passed out. I came to lying on the floor, and

when I opened my eyes Susanne was sitting beside me, holding my hand.

'Kolya?' she said, sounding child-like.

We looked at each other in wonder.

I was overwhelmed by her. She was only a piece of something large that I could only touch through her. She was ready to die.

'Stay a little longer,' I said.

'Why?'

'Because I want to know you.'

She lay down on the floor beside me. I put my arm around her; she nestled into my side. We were silent. It felt like a dream to me, with an undercurrent of motion. I felt some apprehension following her, still unsteady.

'Why aren't you having pain?' I asked her, knowing that it was there, somewhere.

'I took some pills.' She didn't question me about how I knew about the pain. 'I can stand the humiliation, the ugliness, and I've gotten used to being treated like a walking corpse, but I can't really stand the pain. I took three pills, after Jack left, and almost took them all.'

I held her closer to me.

We were dying. I felt as if I'd been plunged into a pool of lukewarm water, unable to breathe, but after a few moments began relaxing. It didn't matter – breathing is easy to give up.

I don't know how long we were there. It seemed to get darker. Perhaps that was the weather – clouds coming between us and the sun. Susanne seemed to cool; I put my arm across her to warm her.

'Kolya,' she whispered.

I forgot to speak.

'I don't want to go back to the hospital.'

'Please, Susanne,' I said. 'I hardly know you yet. I would like more time.' But I felt that I was being unfair in stopping her from going where she really wanted to go.

'Will you come and visit me?'

The hospital. Of all the places in the universe . . . But

what should it matter? I was dying. I could see it, I knew what it was and it didn't frighten me any more. I wondered – if I am there with her, and I watch our breath come and go, if I feel us being eaten with disease, if I feel the world going on without us, if I am there when we leave . . . will my body know that I have died?

'Yes, I'll be there,' I said.

She wrapped her fingers around my wrist, and I could feel my pulse thumping slowly, thinly, against her thumb.

That's when Jack came in.

She helped Susanne to bed. I sat in the rocking chair, torn from Susanne. I don't know how I got the strength to get into the chair, except from a sort of fear of Jack. She gave me a strange look, but she was only surprised at seeing me holding her mother.

The doctor came. I couldn't get to the door. I couldn't move from the chair, so Jack let him in. Then the ambulance came, quietly, without a siren. They rushed through my house, and after a time, carried Susanne through on their stretcher. A squishy bag of clear fluid was held over her. The landlord came to look. I watched Jack talk to him. He nodded, watching them put Susanne into the ambulance. He went back to his house.

Jack looked at me. 'You're some help.'

I tried to turn my palms up to her, but my body was slow.

She moved and spoke wearily. 'I've been up all night. I'm going to the hospital.'

She seemed to be waiting for me to do something. I just stared at the floor. Her keys jangled; she stood at the door. I still had Susanne inside me. I couldn't give her up yet.

'Are you drunk?' she asked.

I shook my head.

'You look drunk. Do you want me to come back, later? I don't know – maybe she's going into surgery. I'll come back and tell you.'

I felt the tiny point of death deep down inside me. Jack was pouring into a funnel, it was going to nothing. How could she continue? Couldn't she see how useless it was to try now?

'Kolya?' she said.

She touched my face; her hands were hot. 'I'll come back later.'

I opened my eyes when the door clicked open. The moonlight came through the living room windows, but I didn't see Jack's face until she turned on the lamp.

'She's all right. It was an ulcer. They sewed it up and she'll be in for a few weeks. Haven't you moved since this afternoon?'

I had been silent too long to answer now. I'd slept and awakened, not remembering the dreams that brought me back. I'd gotten up once to piss, but something made me come back to the chair. I had been waiting, I suppose.

I got and walked to the bedroom. My legs and back were aching and stiff.

Susanne's still alive.

'Kolya, have I done something wrong? Why won't you speak to me? What's the matter with you?'

'You know,' I said, lying on the bed.

She sat down. 'No, I can't even imagine.'

'You know everything you need to know, don't you?'

'What are you talking about? God, I hate it when you talk nonsense!' She pounded her knees with her fists. 'Do you think I've done something to you? What do I know? What?'

She confused me. Invaded me. I have been living my life going to and from classrooms, reading books, fixing myself solitary meals and pots of coffee, writing about things that I think of at random. And now, here comes this woman who is so certain about herself that she thinks she can be certain about *me*. I was sure she knew about me. Miller told her everything, I suspected. All I have to do is hand her the right words and she has my brain on a platter.

Jack took a deep breath and looked to the ceiling, as if for help. 'I've tried to be honest. I've tried to tell you how I feel about things. And you – you won't let me in. Why can't you think about how I feel?' She crossed her arms. 'I want to love you, but you won't let me in, you won't let me help.'

How can it matter any more?

She leaned over me and kissed me on my mouth. Some of Jack trickled down into me, thawing what Susanne had frozen.

I still live.

I reached for her. Oh, God, she was warm, she was lovely. She was sweet and whole and so unlike me. I loved her. I kissed her face and she laughed a little. But then I was exhausted. Couldn't keep my eyes open, so I let her rest on me.

A long time passed. I stroked her hair.

'I have things to tell you,' I said.

'I know.'

'How do you know?'

'Because it shows. You never talk about some things, and a certain expression crosses your face now and then that I know means something is hurting you.'

I believed her. How could I doubt her, or think her capable of conspiracy against me? But how, where to begin? I decided to tell her the 'real' part, so I said, 'I was treated . . . when I was a kid – eleven, twelve, until I was in high school. They said I was a paranoid schizophrenic.' There. I had said the beginning.

'Oh.'

It was worse than she had expected, I could sense that. But I held her and kissed her hair and rubbed her arms a while. She was afraid of me. My heart pounded and my mouth was dry. I was nervous of her, of saying the wrong things.

'Paranoid?' she finally said.

'I swear to you that I wasn't. It's hard to describe what it is, but I have never been a schizophrenic.' I sat up, propped myself on one elbow and looked into the face barely visible in the darkness. 'I am not paranoid. I was a sensitive kid, and different, and no one liked me much. I still don't have a lot of friends, though I do have some. You know that. Now, it's simply because I keep to myself.'

She still tried the label on me. 'Tell me more about it.'

'All right. My mother had a hard time fitting into the family and I wasn't exactly the comfort she had expected. I was one of *them*. I understand why I was an odd child. I still didn't speak English well when I started school – just well enough to get along. But I was different. You know how school children are. It never got better. One day, my mother and teacher were talking about me and I threw a book at Miranda – my mother – and that's why they sent me to a psychiatrist. He made me sick. That was his business. It's simple.'

'No, these things aren't simple.'

I shrugged. 'I didn't understand anything but the culture of my family, which consisted of four people. I was wound tightly into that. The family, the family. The word still brings to me feelings of love and rebellion. I hate them and I love them. I hate to see my father, yet I love him more than any human on earth.' I waved my hand in the air, wishing I could erase the word hate. 'This sounds as if I am giving you reasons for something – but that something doesn't even exist.'

'So,' she said slowly. 'You don't think you were schizophrenic?'

'No. I won't say that I am like you, that I have a completely sound and normal mind, but I'm not crazy.'

'And what about the people looking for you?' she asked. 'What about that?'

'My great-uncle was a criminal. Every now and then someone tries to research it but the family doesn't want to talk about it. Would you?'

'No, I suppose not. Especially if I was as close to my family as you are.' She smiled. 'Is that it? Why didn't you tell me that? I was beginning to think that you were wanted by the FBI or something, or that you might really be a spy.' She hugged me. 'Oh, Kolya, don't you feel better now? It's so much better to tell everything and have it in the open.'

We clung to each other. I thought that she had fallen

asleep after a time and tried to move carefully; my arm began to tingle under her.

'Kolya?'

'Hmmm?'

'What about that night?'

'What night?'

'When you screamed in the kitchen?'

'Oh.'

And now she has doubts. She will remember and be watching. Maybe she'll even fear for her life. I touched her hair. 'I had a nightmare, love, that's all.'

She nodded, then slept.

18 April

The next question came as I brushed my teeth in the morning, getting ready for school.

'You don't like me working for Dr Miller, do you?'

I spat into the sink. 'Did I say that?' I spoke into the drain.

'No, but I've always gotten this feeling when I talked about him . . . ' she said. 'You're afraid of psychologists, aren't you?'

'Listen, Jack, it's better just to let this go. Don't think about it. And don't talk to Miller about it. It's none of his business, is it?'

'How awful it must have been!' She hugged me from behind, resting her cheek on my back.

I looked in the mirror at my grey eyes. How like Mikhail he looks, how like Mikhail, they said.

'Kolya, I've done something that I have to tell you about.'

'What's that?' I wiped my face off with a towel, but when I looked in the mirror, it was still there. What was Jack talking about?

'I've ordered a telephone for you.'

'What!' I turned to her.

'I'll pay for it. I just thought that since I spend so much time here it would be better to have a phone, in case . . . ' As I looked at her, I realized how strained and tired she was. And now afraid of me. I was glad to have had a sip of vodka because I didn't really want to know how she felt.

'It's all right,' I said.

We saw each other in our reflections in the mirror. She took my arm and leaned against me. 'Another thing?'

'What's that?' I could see that she hesitated on this one. Something big. I felt uneasy, looked away from her reflection.

'May I stay with you while Mother's in hospital? I don't really want to go home.'

Stay? Another person in the house all the time. Someone *with* me. I felt panic. I know it showed because she immediately let go of my arm and turned away. But this is Jack. I like Jack. I intend to tell her the truth some day, and what other reason than because I want her to be mine, to be with me. Am I going to live like this for ever?

She was in the hallway. I turned. 'Jack, Susanne Elizabeta, where are you going?'

She just waved a hand back at me and walked toward the kitchen.

I followed her. She was in tears by the end of the hallway. I took her and held her, hoping she would look at me, but she hung her head. 'What's the matter?'

'I'm so confused, I'm sorry,' she said, sniffing, turning her face sideways.

'Jack, listen to me, I've never, never let anyone even spend an entire night with me until you. Do you believe that?'

She lifted her face then. 'You haven't?'

'No.' I wiped the tears off her face. 'I think it might be all right if you stay. We'll try it, okay?'

She smiled tentatively. 'I shouldn't have asked.'

I felt so tender toward those glistening eyes and meek smile. I kissed her, and decided that I should be truthful with her about what it might be like to stay with me. 'I don't know how it will work. I'm a solitary sort of person, and I may send you away into another room to leave me alone or go off for a walk or something every now and then. If you know that ahead of time, it won't be so awful when it happens, right?'

She nodded. 'Or if you want to stay with someone . . .' Her eyes disappeared from my view, and the top of her head tucked under my chin.

'There's no one else.'

'But you stayed out all night the other night . . . ' she said.

'I was alone.' I hugged her. 'Do you believe me?'

'I don't know.'

'Jack.'

She looked up at me.

'I love you,' I said, and it was a tremendously frightening three words to get out. Is that because I wasn't sure of myself? Or her? Or what it means? I have no idea what it really means to say these words, but I felt them. I said them just as my mind always heard them said in novels. Oh, how like a fictional man I felt, how disbelieving that this was *me*. And how terrified I was that it wasn't really true, that she loved me and I really felt nothing, nothing at all.

Everything changed suddenly as soon as she said, 'Oh, Kolya, I love you, too.'

We stood together for a very long time, just holding each other and whispering as if we'd just discovered each other at that moment.

22 April

I promised her, didn't I?

I have never ever been in a hospital since the first few days of my life. It is dangerous, even for the strongest, like my father. My mother began to hate me the day I was born because Papa would not come to be with her. She found the mild Sasha more stubborn about it than she could have imagined. This could have been the first thing he ever refused her. I was certainly no consolation – a thin, sweating baby who apparently screamed whenever awakened, having a low-grade fever the first week of my life.

Day One of Jack's stay with me we had an argument. She rose, bathed, went to the hospital that morning. When she returned, I was reading (*Madame Bovary*). She stood in the doorway.

'My mother wants to see you.'

I was prickled with a sense of Jack's meaning behind the words – a faint sort of accusation, a feeling that if she said it in a certain way, she could get a reaction from me. I know that I had promised Susanne, but that was in another state of mind. There had been her death wish in me, a reckless conquered world in me. Now, I was alive and warm with Jack, the chill had been taken out of my bones. I was cold with dread of going to the hospital.

'Yes,' I said. 'Perhaps tomorrow.'

'I think it would be better if you went today. She is anxious to see you.'

Again, a little accusation.

I felt apprehensive. Or was it Jack? I didn't want to talk about it, but had to clear the air. 'What are you thinking?'

'I don't know,' she said, turning away. 'I guess I wonder why she wants to see you more than her own family.' She leaned against the doorjamb and wouldn't look at me. 'Guess I know why.'

'Why's that?'

'Because you aren't involved.'

I didn't dispute that with her, though a cry sounded inside me at being excluded. 'I talk to her,' I said. 'You can, too.'

'It's not the same, is it?'

'I don't know. I don't know what is the same or different for her.'

'You did talk to her the other day, didn't you?' Jack asked.

'A little.'

'Then are you going to see her?'

'Yes, I will.'

'Why don't you want to?'

I sat up on the bed, closed my book irritably. 'I don't like hospitals.'

She nodded and walked into the living room. Apparently, she was not going to be easy to have around in that mood. I went to the kitchen and opened my cupboard. Jack stood behind me. I took my bottle down and poured out a small measure of vodka.

'Kolya, please don't.'

Holding on to the glass, holding on to my patience, I was thinking that we'd already made a dreadful mistake. 'I know you're right for your reasons, but leave me alone.' I drank it down.

'So I will,' she said and was out the door.

I went back to my book, but it was no longer as interesting. I wrote a little. I opened my chemistry text.

Jack returned after nearly two hours. She came to me and snuggled up. 'I love you,' she said.

We held each other, and eventually made love. I was amazed with her, amazed that she loved me, and amazed that I was glad that she returned. I looked at her face, toyed with her hair. We talked about big things, little things, supper and the Ivory Coast. Then we took a bath together.

I decided to go with her for the afternoon visit. I had to eventually anyway, and felt the strength of her loving me; that would protect me against a lot – I thought at the time.

As Jack dressed, I drank to the point of being a little high, then refilled my pocket flask.

I grew more and more nervous as we drove to the hospital, but we talked about politics, then about a local character we spotted on the street. Jack was in a good mood. In the parking lot, there were little old ladies and men getting out of cars all around us, using their three-legged canes, their walkers, or being guided along by their middle-aged children. All visiting the dying, I know. And I walked right into that.

My heart started pounding as we walked up the steps, increased on the elevator. As we moved down the corridor of the surgical ward (how like and unlike television it was – what clutter, what noise) I let go of Jack's hand, fearing that she would ask me why I was trembling.

Susanne's room was a double; she had the bed by the window. Her aged roommate slept hard. Paul and Julie were already there, but we didn't seem to interrupt any conversation.

Susanne looked awful. A tube came out of her nose, was taped onto her cheek, and ran down into a bottle of brownish liquid in a machine that made a low milking noise. Her hair was flattened on one side. As unseeing as if someone's invisible fingers held them open while she slept on, her eyes were dulled with drugs, bloodshot and glassy.

'Julie,' she said hoarsely, 'let Kolya sit here. You . . . ' she took a breath, 'sit here.' And she touched the bed beside her.

I took the soft, vinyl-covered chair. I put my hands in my pockets. I had to stop the trembling, but a terrible chill ran through my shoulders and back. I felt that my neck was trembling, too.

The room was hot, the sun streamed in over a window ledge, through a forest of plants – some fresh, some already looking a little wilted. Julie smiled at me as she settled on the foot of the bed. Paul sat in a chair against the wall and, after greeting us, seemed to be searching for something to say. Jack stood beside her father, her hair hanging down in braids. She gave me an encouraging look.

'How do you feel?' I asked Susanne.

She shook her head. 'Let's not talk about that.'

'Veronica called this morning,' Paul said. 'I forgot to tell you. She sends her love.'

Susanne nodded slowly, as if she had to, but whoever she

was, Veronica didn't seem to have much effect on Susanne. Paul began to tell a story about Veronica and her husband, which I couldn't really follow. Only Julie seemed to be paying attention. When Paul's voice stopped, I made an obligatory smile.

The curtain between the beds was pulled, but the woman made noises in her sleep, reminding us that she was there. The steam radiator clanged occasionally. Typically institutional – because it wasn't yet summer, the heat must be on, yet the room was uncomfortably warm. I couldn't take my jacket off – I was too weary to move.

I wanted to close my eyes. I wanted to slide down in the chair and close my eyes.

'I'm glad you came to see me,' Susanne said.

'I said I would.'

For just a moment, I forgot the others in the room as we looked at each other. It was still there. I remembered it, and couldn't turn away from it. Susanne's eyelids drooped, then closed, and I was alone for a second. Then someone spoke, I don't remember who or what was said.

The minutes went by like that. Susanne would open her eyes and look at me, someone spoke briefly, conversation without sequence. A sentence here, a reply, then nothing.

Susanne's bed caught fire. She didn't see, nor did Julie. Julie leaned back, her palms in the flames, but she seemed to feel nothing. I looked to Jack for help, but the wall Jack stood against was aflame, too. Paul sat stiffly in his chair, apart from the fire.

I was in trouble. I knew it. Even insensible of what was coming to me, I could feel the effects of waking nightmares rolling over me. I had stopped shivering and now trickles of sweat ran in my collar, sleeves, down my sides, and the vinyl chair was getting damp.

The curtain caught fire. I thought of the sick old woman on the other side, sleeping on. Would she catch fire, too, or was it only what lay in my vision?

'Jack,' I said, but how could I tell her how helpless I was to stop it? 'We have to go.'

135

The flames from the bed came near me; I couldn't move back from them.

Susanne opened her eyes and looked at me. Her hair was on fire, but she smiled. 'I'm glad you came,' she repeated.

Sweat dripped into my ear, tickling me, but I couldn't lift my hand to my head.

I couldn't see details any more, the brightness of the fire was like sun in my eyes. Faces went grey. Someone came into the room, touched the blazing curtain. It was a nurse; I could see the white uniform. She lifted her arms, walked around the bed. I had to close my eyes. I couldn't hang on any longer, keeping a normal expression.

'Jack?' Susanne's voice said far, far away, 'would you get me a little ice? I can have some ice.'

I opened my eyes, but I couldn't see anything but orange light. 'It's the fire,' I said to myself because I knew what it was and it helped me to say it.

'What?' Jack said. 'Kolya?'

I closed my eyes again but the orange light came through my eyelids. I smelled the lake.

The lake. I've never smelled it before but I knew that's what it was. It was cool. I took a deep breath.

Jack touched my head. Her hands were ice and burned me. 'Christ, he's hot! Julie, get someone. Kolya, what's the matter?'

I waited. It's all I could do. Someone came and told me to open my eyes. I couldn't see the woman whose voice was in front of my face. My sleeve got rolled up, my blood pressure taken. I started shaking again with the cold touch of their hands.

'Can you hold a thermometer in your mouth?'

I opened my mouth. I was startled by the sliver of ice sliding under my tongue.

'Well, he's hot, we do know that, don't we?' said the voice.

'What's the matter?'

'Let me get a wheelchair, we'll take him down to emergency.'

'Get me out,' I said, but couldn't think of the English words so they didn't listen to me. Think, Kolya, how do you say . . . how do you say . . . ? 'Please,' I said. 'Take me home, Jack.'

But she didn't.

There was a time when I was burning. I felt the flames all over me, inside me. Then I felt water all around me, coming up into my mouth as I tried to get up out of the lake. There isn't really a lake, I thought, but it seemed that there was nothing under me but water. I tried to swim, to keep my head above water. I could see the house from the lake – there is the birch tree, there is the barn, I thought, and I am drowning in the lake.

Someone was holding my hand and keeping me from sinking.

I woke up after a blank period, sore and exhausted, and freezing cold. Even though I had a blanket over me, underneath the stretcher was cold. I was in a small room with thick walls and a cart of instruments and bandages by the bed. A nurse sat in a chair writing on a pad of paper. My wrists were tied to the sides of the stretcher, my legs strapped down.

'I'm cold,' I said.

The nurse looked up. 'Oh, you're awake.' She put her writing down on the chair as she stood. She picked up an electronic thermometer and put the probe under my tongue. She untied me.

Finally, she took the thermometer out. 'Are you feeling better?'

'Yes. I'd like to go home now.'

'I'm not sure you should do that. We'll see what the doctor says. You had a pretty high fever. You were hopping around, so we had to tie you down,' she said apologetically. She unplugged the cold damp thing I was lying on.

'I'd like to see my girlfriend, Jack. Is she out there?'

'I'll see.'

The nurse left. I could hear noises outside the door, but this room was safe, somehow isolated enough to be all right.

My muscles were so sore I could hardly move. Tried to sit up but my arm shook badly.

Never again. I will never again be found in a hospital. It had been difficult years ago when I went to an out-patient clinic to have a vasectomy; I hated that on a different level. This was dangerous.

Jack peeked in the door, then came in cautiously. 'You all right?'

'Well, yes.' I held out my hand to her.

'You had a seizure,' she said, looking at me as if she'd just seen me for the first time in years.

'Oh. Didn't know that. Well, I suppose I guessed. It's okay, Jack, I just need to get out of here.'

'You had a fever of a hundred and seven point four.'

'Pretty hot. Fever's gone now.'

She rubbed my arm. 'This has happened to you before, hasn't it?'

'How would you know that?' I asked, treasuring the feel of her hands on my arm.

'Because you aren't surprised.'

She waited for an answer and I thought about how much to reveal. 'Yes, it's happened before. And if I don't get out of here, it will happen again. Believe me, Jack, and help me leave.'

She nodded. 'When did it happen before?'

'I'll tell you later. When we're home.' Home. I imagined my house, the mattresses on the floor and the woolly blanket over me, soft pillows. I imagined Jack there, too, reading a book in bed, and me – warm, content, reading alongside her. I imagined falling asleep there, because that was the strongest desire I had – to sleep.

She stroked my hair.

'Susanne Elizabeth,' I said, feeling sleepier and sleepier.

'What?' she whispered.

The doctor came in. 'Well, Nicholas, you're awake, huh? How are you feeling?'

'Fine.'

'I'll bet you are.' He was big and carried a broad-

138

shouldered presence into the room. He sat in the chair that the nurse had been in and he, too, had a clipboard of papers to write on. 'Have you ever had a seizure before?'

'All I want to do is to go home. I'm fine now.'

'Well, I'm not sure about that. I'd like to put you in overnight. We're running some blood tests, and I'd like to take some X-rays of your head.'

'No.'

The doctor shrugged. 'Your student insurance will pay for it.'

'I know. I don't want you to X-ray me. I'm leaving. Would you find my clothes, Jack?' I said.

'Look, I don't think you realize how sick you might be.'

Oh, I do. 'I'm refusing treatment. Nothing personal. I know I'll be fine. You'll find that I have a high blood alcohol content.' I wanted to give him something for his trouble. 'I know what happened and it won't happen again.'

'What happened?' he asked.

'None of your business.'

'I don't think it's that simple.'

'No, it isn't.'

'Look, this is for your own sake.'

'I'm refusing treatment. I'm refusing X-rays. I'm refusing to stay,' I said. Jack had found my shirt and jeans and handed them to me.

The doctor bristled at me. I could sense his frustration. I was probably the most interesting thing he'd handled for a week or so and he was disappointed. But I felt good. I wished that I'd been able to say these things as a child. God, how great to be an adult!

'You may have a serious problem. Untreated, it would be extremely dangerous. You had a fever . . .'

'I know. But it's only dangerous to me. I just can't stay.'

'All right,' he said, holding his hands up in the air. He then picked up his clipboard and left the room. I could imagine him as a high school kid, angry after fumbling the football in an important game.

Jack said nothing. She helped me sit up and dress. I was shaky, but feeling better. Triumphant.

The nurse came in with a wheelchair. 'Leaving us, huh?'

They helped me into the chair. When I tried to put weight on the soles of my feet, they shuddered and wouldn't hold me. I sat in the chair, trying to hold my head up. My lip was sore. I suddenly realized that I must have bitten it.

Jack wheeled me out into the emergency room. The doctor brought a release for me to sign. I wanted to get out, get away. I could feel others coming at me, floating toward me though the echoing corridor, threatening to liquefy me into another mass of short-circuits.

I heard a voice. She was speaking my language.

'What are you doing to me?' she said. 'Oi, oi!'

'Wait.' I listened. She was so frightened. It could be someone like Grandmama, an old woman alone without language to help her. And then I heard her speak again, and someone spoke back to her impatiently. 'Hold still!'

I felt like weeping. I couldn't stay. I didn't have the strength. I hope she is all right now.

When we got home, I slept through the evening, through the night and woke at 4 a.m. Jack slept. I think I interrupted a dream, but she only stirred a little as I crawled over her.

I was as sore as if I'd carried elephants for two hours; I was having little light flashes behind my eyes, which I'd forgotten as part of the after-effects of seizure. Like flash-bulbs going off inside, yellowing out my sight and making a small popping sound. That would go away in a day or so, after gradual decrease.

I made some coffee, scrambled two eggs, and ate in the kitchen. I was still hungry and thirsty and scrounged through the refrigerator several times. Then I took a cup of coffee and lit a cigarette at my desk and began to scribble here, as is my habit.

Jack rose about seven. 'How are you?' she said sleepily.

'I'm fine.' At that moment, I felt a pop in my head, but other than a blink, I probably showed no outward sign. I put my papers away in the drawer and locked it.

Jack walked zombie-like into the kitchen and poured herself a cup of coffee. Then made another pot. She sat down in the rocker. We were both wrapped in flannel, wearing socks, as the floors were cold. I felt cozy, looking at her dressed that way, and so sleepy.

'You scared the shit outa me yesterday,' she said.

'I'm sorry. I shouldn't have gone to the hospital. I think I'm allergic to something in them.'

'Hmmm.' Jack began to rock. 'What were you writing?'

'Not much.'

'You write a lot. I've noticed that. Stories?'

I shook my head. 'Just things that I think of. Things that happen.'

'A journal,' she said, catching on. She yawned. 'I've tried that now and then. Julie got into my diary when I was still in high school and read some of it to Mom, so that stopped me for a while.'

'Yes,' I said, not wanting to talk about it.

'Don't worry. I'm not going to go looking for it.'

'You'd have to have it translated.'

'Oh. Well, see, nothing to worry about then.' She took a sip of coffee and rocked the chair with her heels. I drank, too. We smiled at each other. 'I'm glad you're all right now,' she said. 'You knew you'd be better, didn't you? I kind of liked seeing you talk to that doctor. He was an unbearable asshole.'

'Really? He just seemed immature to me.'

'That, too.'

She was inquisitive. I felt her questions coming. I got up to get more coffee, and lit another cigarette.

'Kolya?'

'Yes, I'll tell you.'

And, so I did. I told her about first throwing the book at my mother, then the interview with Dr Wall. I was surprised at how things that I'd forgotten came back to me as I talked to Jack about them. I'd never spoken, written, or even thought very deeply about any of it as an adult. I had tried to forget.

First impression: Dr Wall had a brass elephant with pencils and pens sticking out of its back on his desk. I remember how smooth my psychiatrist seemed to me – smooth, slick hair, a soft face and shiny nose, dark blue eyes that he covered with glasses only when he was reading. He wore brown suits a lot. I hated him. I was ten, eleven? He was a compromise worked out between the school and my father.

He asked me why I was angry, and I was trying to remember what my father said about spooning it out carefully. I told him that I was angry because my grandfather was old.

A mark for little Nicholas.

And slowly, I let him know bits about Miranda hating the family, feeling like an outsider, resenting us all.

It looked as though things were going to work out with just a few conversations, and I could be released from these sessions as a repentant child, a victim of culture shock, and suffering acutely from my parents' marital problems.

Then my grandfather got sick.

This part I didn't tell Jack about completely. I told her that I was upset by his illness and, at that time, I had my first seizure. It made everything immensely more complicated, since Dr Wall was ahead of his time in thinking that mental illness is merely a manifestation of physical malfunction. This was still in the era of ghosts and hysteria . . .

I remember the day. I came home from school. It was cold, perhaps early spring, but my father was sitting on the porch wearing his hat and coat. When I got to the porch, he handed me a water glass of wine. 'Drink up, little one,' he said.

He told me gently that old Fyodor Nicholaevich had been taken to the hospital, and that he'd had a stroke. It looked as if he might not live much longer. He'd become unconscious as soon as the neighbor had taken him to the hospital

– Grandmama had been shopping and the neighbor saw him fall in the back yard.

It didn't mean much to me at first. I didn't understand death, and only later, when I understood the difference between a Dal and other people, did I see that the neighbor had innocently and unknowingly killed my grandfather.

My father and I ate dinner alone that night. Neither of us were feeling well; I was a little feverish and Papa was depressed but hiding it from me. I went to bed early. I didn't really understand what was happening.

Until Grandmama came home. I heard the taxicab stop in front of the house, and her coming up the steps, unlocking the door. I got out of bed and peeked through my doorway at her. She sat in the chair, weeping, still wearing her coat and gloves.

'Grandmama,' I said, coming out of my room.

'Nicholas, no!' She looked up at me.

She was afraid of me. That was the first wave. I remember her shocked look, and her hand up, as if to ward me off.

The second wave was grief. It hit me hard. It had a name and that was Fyodor Nicholaevich, and the world seemed to slip out from under me just like that. Thump. I was a stranger, and I was a stranger in a world that was filled with horrible dread.

I don't even remember what happened, myself, but I have gathered that my father didn't know where to turn when I became unconscious, then began to have a seizure. He didn't want me taken to the hospital. He called my psychiatrist.

I was then admitted to the children's ward of the psychiatric hospital, where I had a seizure every night after lights out. And every morning, I awakened an old man, my joints and muscles stiff and sore, my eyes popping with crackling flashes of light. I remember little of that time – months, it was, and then I was transferred to a 'special school' where the seizures became less frequent.

What I remember most was a feeling of having someone's

fist in my stomach all the time. Papa has told me that he visited me, but I didn't know who he was sometimes. I was affected by all the children around me. I had all their diseases – depression, schizophrenia, autism (that's where I lost most of my time) and even some more entertaining neuroses. I was not myself. Nicholas Alexandrovich had disappeared.

The closest thing that I've ever felt could explain it was something I came across years later in a history book. At one period in its history, Poland ceased to exist. The country had been carved up and given away to all those surrounding it; the Poles existed legally as Germans, or Russians, but Poland was gone. (But restored eventually.)

That struck me then as an exact reverse of what had happened to me. The name for me did exist, yet the self had been given away to the neighbors.

Since I wasn't a dangerous child, I was allowed to go home for visits. My grandfather had died only weeks after I was taken away, so it was just Grandmama and Papa. In the summer of my thirteenth year, I was allowed a long visit, perhaps two weeks. I slowly came back to myself in that time. I had enough sense to know that I was better at home. Papa refused to let me go back. Dr Wall saw improvement, too, and gave in, as long as I continued seeing him weekly.

What a tough shell I developed in those years of talking to him! I knew him far better than he could ever know me. I knew how to distract and manipulate him. I knew how to protect myself. And I drank a lot. One day, when I was sixteen, he said, 'Well, Kolya, I think that there comes a point when a therapeutic relationship comes to a standstill. I want to ask you one thing: do you feel that you are a functioning human being?'

That was the only moment that I ever felt he respected me.

'Yes,' I said.

'Then I will let you go unless you want to go on seeing me.'

Rather cruelly, after all those years of him prodding at

me for what he had always felt was my own good, I left him. I stood, and without a handshake or thank you, I walked out.

I told Jack most of this, but in a guarded way so that she could get no hint of our family being different.

I told her my life story without mentioning Mikhail, though he was there, in it all.

23 April

Monday. We both went to classes, but I was still feeling a little ill. Dropped by the library to tell Patricia that I wouldn't be in to work. I said it too quickly, too certainly, and she cross-examined me for ten minutes, looking at my eyes (which were popping only occasionally), asking all about my symptoms, everything short of putting her perfumed hand on my fevered brow. I came up with a list that sounded like dysentery, smallpox, influenza, strep throat and multiple sclerosis. She let me go after she gave me the name and number of her internist.

I met Jack in the student lounge and we went home. She insisted on fixing a big meal. She pointed to my ribs and told me that I looked tubercular more than anything after I told her about Patricia. She seemed so delighted to hear an account of such an ordinary thing as a conversation with my boss. We ate, drank some wine, and just talked with each other. She was lovely and I fell more in love than ever. Oh, I know that she was treating me gently for many reasons, but she was loving me, too.

I've never felt this. I've never told someone so much. I've never trusted. I've never felt so safe that a woman would not take me away from myself.

We just sat in the kitchen, holding hands and talking.

About six, Paul and Julie came by. Paul! Yes, come right into my house, I thought resentfully, but wasn't it natural? It made Jack and me seem like an 'us' to have her family visit. They were on their way to see Susanne, and did we want to go? And how was I feeling? He looked around the house, and I knew he was thinking it bare, and also threatening, since there seemed to be more books than furniture.

I told Jack to go ahead, that I would try to do some homework. As soon as she had gone, I sat at my desk here and enjoyed doing nothing for a while. I have just finished reading the main text for English History and clearing off the desk. I'm sleepy, Jack still isn't home, but I'm going to bed.

30 April

It's starting to sink in that next week we have our finals. Today started out all wrong. Late for class. Felt Dr Miller somewhere near at one point and started getting nervous. Wanted a drink. Felt pressure to get this done, remember that, look up things I've missed somehow. Had a chemistry exam on an empty stomach and could only think about getting something to eat.

Went to work. Jack came in and sat at a table close enough that I could glimpse her shoulder and one leg and a great spill of black hair. Patricia must have taken a whole bath in perfume, she just about choked me. Am I being too sensitive to smell and temperature? Patricia also told me that I look worse than ever, told me that I should see her doctor.

When we got home, I was exhausted. Didn't feel like fixing a meal, so I suggested sandwiches. Jack was quiet about it, as if I were shirking a duty. If she only knew how I usually ate, she would think sandwiches very civilized and domestic of me. She was thinking about her mother again.

I could feel the beginning of those grief waves like heat coming off summer asphalt. I opened the cupboard and took a drink.

'Why do you have to drink so much?' she said.

I should have used a glass, it looks better than simply unscrewing the cap and taking a drink.

'Jack, we've talked about this. Just don't start on me.'

'You're going to kill yourself.'

I sighed. I said nothing.

'Oh, now, clam up,' she said.

What on earth had gotten into my even-tempered Jack? I know how I probably appear outside, and she was learning more and more about the inside without knowing the core. Perhaps she didn't love me any more, knowing the fraction of the tangled mess that is me. And she's worrying about her mother. On top of this, finals loom. A tough time for her.

'Are you going to see your mother this evening?' I asked.

'Probably. I'm going to get the telephone, too.'

'Oh, the phone.'

'Why don't you want the phone?'

'I didn't say I didn't want it. I've just never had one in my own place. They're awfully noisy.'

Jack rubbed her temples as if she had a headache. 'They're awfully useful, too.'

'All right, that's true.'

'You have so many rules,' she said.

'Rules? What are you talking about?'

'Everything is on your terms. How close or far I can be to you, how you live, how much you drink. You don't compromise.'

'No one's asked me to,' I said, surprised that she would see things that way.

'No.' She looked down at the table and not at me. 'I wouldn't dare. You've made it clear that I'm an intruder here.'

'Jack,' I said, helplessly. I had no defense. 'I love you. I don't mean to hurt you.'

'But . . . ' She toyed with a fork, drawing imaginary lines on the table. Then she just shook her head.

I had known all along that she had uneasy feelings about me – especially when I was drinking. But, until now I didn't understand them very deeply. I had misinterpreted, I had brushed them off the way I have done with other girls who meant much less to me. It has become very easy to become calloused to others' discomfort because I have to live with it like a rock in my shoe. But, suddenly, I was unsure of my understanding of another. I've never felt that way before.

Could it be that I have always interpreted everyone wrongly? I had a dizzying sense of insight and uncertainty.

'Kolya,' she said at last, 'sometimes I'm frightened of you.'

'Of me?' I was surprised again. Someone frightened of *me*? 'I've never been dangerous.' But something deep stirred. Someone in me rose from the dead to listen to her.

'You're powerful somehow. I don't know what parts of you I can touch.'

I had an instinctive knowledge of what she was trying to say at last. There are no answers for it, nothing I can do.

She recognizes me. I can't hide from that any longer. Perhaps she'll forgive me, or perhaps she'll hate me.

3 May

The telephone rang a while ago. It's the first time I've heard the phone ring in my house. I jumped out of my chair.

It was Susanne. 'Is Jack there?'

'I think she's on her way over to see you now.'

'Oh. How are you feeling?' she asked me.

'I'm fine. And you?'

'I'll be going home next week.'

'I will visit you there.'

There was a silence, and a voice in the background. Then Susanne said, 'I'd like that. I'm sorry the hospital made you sick.'

I didn't know what to say. It was uncanny that she would put it that way, as if she knew exactly what had happened.

'How's everything, are you holding on all right?' I asked, feeling that I could return one close comment with another.

'Yeah, I suppose so.' She paused for a moment, but spoke again before I could think of anything to say. 'I think about things you said and that helps me.'

I can't imagine what things she is thinking of.

'Well, here's Jack now. I'll see you later,' she said and we ended there.

5 May

I woke yesterday with an exhilarating sense of freedom. No school for two weeks, no work. And Jack sleeping soundly, dreamlessly, beside me. I picked up the book I'd been reading the night before, Loren Eiseley's biography of Sir Francis Bacon, but got bored with pages and pages of praise without substantial biography. But what can be said about a man whose importance has outlived his facts?

Got out of bed, made coffee, and sat in front of the bookcase looking for a novel to read. I'd read so many of them, had so little interest in the rest, that I decided it was time to go to the bookstore. How I love to read. It must be my natural state – sucking the books dry for all their conflict and power and ideas, my own self-inflicted empathy, not the intrusion of others on my mind, but a genuine sympathy for the characters.

I settled down in the rocker with a book of short stories. Had read most of them, but forgotten some, missed others.

Jack roused herself, spent a few minutes in the bathroom, then pattered out in a T-shirt and panties. She got coffee and sat in my desk chair, sipping.

'Let's go to the movies today,' she said. 'I haven't been to the movies all semester.'

I looked up from my book. 'I hate the movies.'

'Hate them!' She opened her mouth melodramatically.

'Well, I don't hate movies. I hate movie theaters.' All

those people, packed shoulder to shoulder, all of them interpreting their own way. Some having a good time, some having a rotten time. And it's even more confusing if the film attracts children. Or if it's pornography. I went to a triple-X-rated movie once (in younger years), stayed for five minutes, and got the ugliest sort of feelings and left to get good and drunk.

'Do you have agoraphobia?' she asked.

I felt my shirt pocket. She laughed.

'Fear of public places,' she explained.

'Oh. Perhaps a little.'

'Do you feel panicked when you get into a big crowd of people?'

'Mm, well, sometimes. Would you like me to fix breakfast?'

'If you want.' She watched me cross the room. I could see in her eyes that she loves me, so I retraced a few steps and kissed her on the way to the kitchen. She followed and sat down at the table while I broke eggs.

Breakfast was nearly ready when I started to feel depressed and anxious.

'What do you really think happens when someone dies?' Jack asked suddenly.

'Do you mean what do I *believe* happens? Are you asking me a scientific or religious question?'

'I suppose philosophical,' she said, chin in palm.

'I believe that we can't know without trying it out ourselves.' The bottle was in the cupboard right above my left hand. I could just reach in, but there was Jack, watching me lovingly. I would fight it, I didn't want to spoil things.

'It can't be bad, though,' she said, hopefully.

'I don't imagine it can be worse than living. In fact, people seem to remain dead much longer – it can't require as much patience.'

'I love the way you talk.'

'Thank you. I love everything about you,' I said. 'You don't know, little one. I've never wanted anyone around so much. I don't mean to make you sound privileged, that's arrogant. But I want you to know how much . . . '

We smiled at each other. 'I like being here.' And she stretched her arms over her head lazily.

Why don't you stay? I almost asked, but didn't. I couldn't. Stay. Someone living here with me, but that someone would be Jack. Jack's not just someone, she's herself. I like having her here with me. I like waking up with her in my bed, and looking across the room at midday and seeing that she's still here. When she leaves to go somewhere, at first I feel a relief at being alone, but it doesn't last. I start looking at the clock after a time, wondering just how long it will be before she shows up again.

I didn't reach for the bottle this morning because she sat there, and we talked those bad feelings away. Instead, I felt warmth of a different kind.

She loves me. It feels good. I wish I could send it back to her. I wish that she could be as wise about my love as I am about hers. It's an unfair advantage to know her feelings, isn't it? But I'm taking it.

I don't know what will happen in the future. Maybe some day I'll ask her to stay.

We didn't do much the rest of the day – went to the park and ate lunch at the tavern where we had our first date together. From there, we called Gus and Freda and invited them over for the afternoon. Jack also called a friend of hers, Caroline, and we made a party of it. I bought some wine and beer; Jack bought some chips and made some of her chocolate cookies. We just talked and listened to music. I felt comfortable, even around Caroline, whom I don't know very well, although she does spout her opinions as if she's just discovered that she has them.

At one point, Gus and I were in the kitchen, each getting more to drink. He grinned at me. 'Doin' okay?'

'Yes,' I said.

'Heard you were sick a few days ago.'

I raised my eyebrows. 'How did you know that?'

'Jack told me when I came by the other day. You were sleeping. You look all right now. You look almost like what I would call happy.'

I shrugged; I smiled. 'I think I am.'

'Well, some day, maybe you'll be able to recognize it,' Gus said, laughing. 'I'm sure you don't even know what it is yet, you dour old Russian.'

'Gus,' I said, patiently, putting my hand on his shoulder. 'Many times I've told you this.' (I thickened up my accent to sound just like Papa.) 'I *am* Russian, but I am *an* American.'

This always amuses my friend Gus.

'Look,' I said, pulling out my wallet. I showed him my credit cards.

'But have you used them?'

'Once.' I stuffed them back into my pocket.

Freda peeked into the kitchen to see what we were chuckling about. Gus said, 'The truck driver said, "I thought you were taking those penguins to the zoo!" So, the guy says to the truck driver, "We've been to the zoo, now we're going to the movies." '

'I don't get it.' I put my arm around Freda. 'He's not funny.'

'It's a good joke,' Freda said seriously.

I have never had such a cheerful evening with friends. After they left, Jack and I went to bed and made love.

7 May

Susanne called. Called me. It was well after midnight last night. Jack woke up and came with me to the phone, but I answered.

'Hello,' I said, and remembered in my sleepiness to speak English, '*Hello?*'

'Kolya, this is Susanne.'

A strange thrill went through me at hearing her voice.

'Are you all right?'

'I'm in pain.'

'Won't the nurse give you something?'

'She said it's too soon.' Susanne began to cry. 'I went crazy today. And I'm sorry to wake you up.'

'It's all right,' I said. I knew that she was calling *me* right then, and didn't offer the phone to Jack. 'Maybe your medicine isn't working.' I was repeating something I'd heard Jack say the afternoon before.

'Kolya,' she said, her voice breaking. 'I want to let go.'

I didn't know what to say. Jack was leaning toward me, expectantly. She knew it was her mother. 'I understand,' I said.

'I don't know how yet.'

'When you know, then it will be time.' I wanted to see her. I wanted to go and get her out of that place and put her gently someplace soft and sweet.

'I'm sorry I called,' she said.

'Don't be. I want you to, if you need to.'

She wept and I just held the phone, helpless. How I wanted to see her! I have never had such a powerful urge to see someone.

I was getting dangerous interference from Jack.

'Susanne, here's Jack, she wants to talk to you.'

'Oh, I didn't know she was there.'

I felt something strange and unreal tugging at me from inside. 'Hold on,' I said ambiguously.

'Yeah,' she said softly.

I handed the phone to Jack. I didn't hear what Jack said, but headed straight for the bottle. I was going to be in trouble. Already, I was hot. Christ, I was hot. My legs trembled, my hands shook. I drank a lot.

'Okay, Mother, see you tomorrow.'

Jack came to the kitchen door. 'That's what I thought,' she said, and went back into the bedroom.

I sat in the rocker for a long, long time, trying to hold on to myself. Jack was awake. I knew she was tossing and turning, doubled up in an agony of grief. I couldn't leave

153

her like that, but I wasn't feeling any better. I was growing weaker with fever.

Finally, I went into the bedroom and found my clothes and dressed as quietly as I could.

'What are you doing?' Jack asked, sitting up in bed.

'I'm going for a walk.'

'Now?'

'I have to.'

She lay down. 'Why did she call you?' Jack asked.

'She called here,' I said.

'Kolya, come and hold me.'

Oh, I swear that I wanted to; I couldn't touch her. 'Little Susanne Pavlovna, believe me, I love you, but I have to go.'

'Are you going to the hospital?'

'No, my love, I am not. I have just decided that I'm going to go and visit my father.'

'Your father? But there aren't any buses until morning.'

'I'll be back for supper. In fact, I will fix supper. Promise.'

She was silent, but I could hear in her breathing that she was weeping. Oh, Jack, if I could tell you. I stood over her. She reached her hand up to me. I took it and kissed it.

'You're hot.'

'Yes.'

'Be careful.'

I walked to the bus station and took the first bus to Denver this morning.

Alexander Fyodorovich's apartment waits for company. He has two big comfortable chairs, a small round coffee table between them, an eternally ready pot of coffee, cookies, potato chips, a double bed, more brands of booze than he drinks himself. Hardly a soul visits him. I looked around his apartment, guiltily thinking how long it had been since I had visited.

'What are you going to do?' Papa asked me. He lit up a cigar. We filled the room with blue smoke.

I leaned back in the chair, trying to get comfortable.

Those chairs are too *damn* cozy. 'I'm going back, of course. Just had to leave for a while.'

Papa nodded. 'I used to leave for a walk in the middle of the night sometimes.'

'I know. I remember.'

'You didn't get much sleep as a boy, Nicholas.'

I smiled. 'I had a dream about Miranda the other night.'

'Oh?' Papa seemed to shrug. He topped me. 'I saw her.'

'*Saw* her?'

He nodded. 'I saw her in a department store. She didn't see me – or didn't seem to.'

'Papa . . . '

'No, it's fine,' he said. 'It wasn't just you. She wouldn't have stayed much longer anyway.' He smiled vaguely. 'When I married her, I was so happy at first. I didn't have to be lonely, and I *like* women. I really like their company, I like to have them. But then, I started to see how the family ate away at our marriage. I didn't have enough money, or enough strength to get away from them. But Mama wasn't nice to her – well, she wasn't mean, but she made it clear that we were living in her home. And Miranda was such a strain. Couldn't talk around her. Father wanted me to tell her. I was so afraid that she would leave me if she knew about the family. But then I put my seed there . . . I wanted you more than anything in the world then. And when it came to choosing every day between what you needed and Miranda wanted, I chose you. I had to, and I chose you every time. I did – still do – love you more than anything in this world. God help you, Kolya, if you ever have to make choices like that.'

I reached over and squeezed my father's forearm. We sat silently for a time.

'Kolya, I think you should stay away from the family until the woman dies.'

'I don't think you understand, Papa.'

'I do.'

'Jack's part of her family, and I . . . '

I didn't have to explain. I knew he felt envy, too. Once he

told me that he would never go back and live with his mother again. After I'd become old enough to be independent of him, he'd decided to live alone because, perhaps one of these days, he might meet someone and she might want to stay with him. He'd learned that in America women don't want men who live with their mothers once they are grown. Why couldn't it have been Papa instead of me who has fallen in love? He *needs* it; I don't. It just happened to me.

When I got home, it seemed as if Jack had been crying. She greeted me with a tight hug. 'I'm glad you're home,' she said. 'I missed you.'

'I'm glad you're here,' I said, then I fixed supper.

10 May

The house seems very empty now. I didn't expect this feeling. The only light on is at my desk. I've cleared away all my notebooks for the semester, filed papers, put the textbooks I'm keeping into the bookcases. Sold the chemistry text, can't imagine reading it again.

I thought after these two or more weeks that Jack might want to stay, at least on a part-time basis. But she packed up all her books and clothes and left me. 'I think you're jealous of my family!' she said, and laughed.

But I didn't laugh. I think I've suddenly lost what little sense of humor I have.

She's good for me. Makes me do things that I've never wanted to do, and they don't turn out so badly after all. The other night we went to a movie. Saw a comedy at the late show, not too many people there. I had forgotten what it was like – the darkness, the gigantic images, the complete involvement. The sound was so real. I lived the movie so intensely that I forgot to laugh at the painful humor. Felt like crying, but Jack laughed, and I sensed her wit about it, and suddenly it *was* funny. Was exhausted afterwards. The next day, I continued to think about it as if it had all happened to me; I asked Jack about something that had occurred in the movie and she couldn't remember. I was amazed that she could shrug the experience off so easily.

Well, soon Jack starts to work regularly for Dr Benjamin Miller. I had forgotten to worry about him while she was here, but I am getting worried about it again now.

How am I doing?

I still have the Dreadful Bad Thoughts sometimes, too.

I was musing on the effect visiting Europe would have on Jack, how it would help her to be well-traveled, since it doesn't ever hurt anyone, I suppose. But I started imagining her talking about her trip afterwards and got a strange insight to what she might sound like – 'I saw the most interesting thing in Paris, etc.' The charming, hard-working tourist's insights to another culture coming out of her mouth, incorporated into her experiences, but unassimilated. Jack is so weighted in the center of her world. She wears the right clothes, has the right parents and upbringing, has good common sense and an estimate of her own value. She is Jack to the core.

What of the places one goes and can't discuss later in life? Would she ever have an experience only hinted at darkly, obliquely, that smelled of smoke, whiskey, sex, and a temper? Would she ever get her fingernails torn clawing her way out of a situation that would shake her awake, or would she only be scraping pottery out of the earth to look at remnants of some long-dead culture?

I want to rattle Jack sometimes. I want to make her stop standing where she stands, and be something else entirely. I want to see her brow darkened with things on her conscience, I want her to have regrets, an unchecked impulse, passion.

She can explain everything to me, everything she does, everything I do, and I lose, I lose every time.

14 May

Jack went to Denver with Caroline to shop. She called and asked me if I wanted to go with her and visit my grandmother while they shopped, but I was feeling too lazy to travel. I didn't want to sit in the car with them for hours, listening to them chatter about people and things in which I have no interest.

So I waited for an hour.

Then I called Susanne and asked her if I could visit.

She sat in the living room with the drapes wide, the door opened. I don't know why I had expected her to be sitting in darkness. The house seemed transformed by air and light, and she sat so delicately in it.

I didn't have any alcohol before I went to see her. I didn't want to. I wanted her company undiluted.

A big clock with a pendant ticked, a pair of house finches sang outside the window. I remember this because it was difficult to start the conversation. She served cold tea with oranges. We talked about her health for a few minutes – she is stable – but got bored with that.

She talked about travel as something she regretted missing in her life. 'Hopefully, Jack will make it to Europe next summer. She's always wanted to go.'

I didn't want to tell her what I'd been thinking. I didn't want to talk about why Jack hadn't gone this summer. I knew.

Susanne looked waif-like. She wore a scarf on her head, but her forehead was so high, the hair peeking out from under the scarf and as wispy as a 2-year-old's. Her eyes are growing larger every time I see her. Large and brown. I remember the first time I saw those eyes in the photograph, and the spell hasn't changed.

She asked me if I'd ever thought about visiting the Soviet Union. I said, no, I always felt that I would have too much trouble getting out again because of my accent. They would assume that's where I belonged.

'What was your family farm like?' she asked.

And I told her about the house, made of wood and stone, two stories with rooms added on every now and then. My grandfather's brother, Stepan, had built another room for himself and his family only months before the end. The house was surrounded by white birch trees and a small lake lay beyond the road. I told her about being able to howl and make the wolves answer on summer evenings.

I felt her slipping back and forth in her attention; I was only a distraction. She watched me carefully, however. Feeling free to talk, I told her more about the lake. I told her how crystal clear it was, how cool, and that you could see the rocks, the weeds, and fish all around the edges, then it became so deep that there seemed to be no bottom. I nearly put my hand in the lake. I nearly felt the bones which are still there, reaching up toward the shore. Susanne listened, and she could see the lake, too.

We sat in silence then, both of us trying to breathe. I, too, had lost interest in my words.

I wanted to take her somewhere, dress her in something soft and dark, kiss her, smooth her hair. Then put my hand on her heart and stop it painlessly.

Then I would close her eyes and I would know what there is to know.

I'll miss those eyes. Will anyone miss mine?

21 May

I am feeling a little bit anxious. Jack has been working with Dr Miller for a week now. I haven't seen much of her because she says she's tired but getting used to doing math and researching all day. I guess it's not an easy job. She also seems distant and impatient with me.

I think she's found me out. She's finally catching on that I'm not worthy of her. I seem to irritate her now, especially with my drinking. I haven't been as charming as I could be, I suppose. Must try harder. What was I like before, when she loved me so much? What was I doing right then? I can't remember now.

Part of this is that I have been seeing Susanne every day. We haven't told anyone that we meet – sometimes just for coffee and a sandwich in a truck stop down the highway, where we won't see anyone we know. It's not that we're doing anything underhand, it's just easier not to say anything than try to explain. She just wants to be with me. And I with her. Twice, she has come to my house. Once, she had barely gone when Jack dropped by.

I wonder what Jack would think of it, but it's nothing really to be defensive about. We rarely even speak.

We merely sit and exist side-by-side. It's a great comfort to her.

29 May

I have to reconstruct. I'm foggy about a few days.

Jack visited me one day and asked me what was wrong with me. I didn't know anything was wrong, but she talked about ordinary things (she said) and I couldn't quite follow – not that I didn't understand her, but I couldn't imagine *why* she wanted to talk about these things. They seemed so trivial.

I started to have a pain in my side which nagged at me. Not a bad pain. A *stitch*, it's called, I can't catch my breath sometimes. It's still here in my ribs, but not nagging so today.

And one of those nights, he came in and tried to give me his candle, but I just stared him down, then he left.

Didn't drink at all for days.

Last night I woke up in a sweat. My own, I think. I was terrified of being alone. For the first time in my life, I really felt lonely and afraid. I called Jack. The phone rang and rang then there was a voice. I thought it was Jack, but whoever said, 'Just a minute.'

I waited for a long time. Then, she picked up the phone and said, 'Kolya, what's wrong?'

'Please come here.'

'What's wrong?'

'I don't know. I just want you to come over.'

'Jesus Christ, Nicholas, it's four-thirty and you scared me outa my wits. I thought something had happened. Are you drunk?'

I tried to remember why I called and it seemed so useless.

'Kolya, listen. I don't know what you'll think of this, and maybe this isn't the right time to talk about it, but I think you should talk to someone about yourself. You're getting to be too much even for me to try to understand.'

'No, Jack, I'll be all right. I just want to have you here.'

'Don't you understand? You have problems that I can't help you with. You won't tell me in the first place what's going on with you, so what can I do? I can check with some people at school about someone for you to see, not like that Dr Whatever that you saw as a kid – someone good. Someone to help you with your drinking, everything.'

My mouth was bitter with her words.

'Are you there?' she said. 'Kolya?'

'I think I'm dying.'

'Don't be dramatic. You're depressed. It's obvious. About what, I don't know. But you're not dying.'

'Susanne, don't hang up.'

'Please don't call me that. I hate it when you call me that. Go to sleep. I'll see you at lunch tomorrow. Tomorrow is the first day of classes, remember?'

'Please come over.'

'Not right now, Kolya. It's okay, you'll be okay. You aren't feeling suicidal or anything stupid like that, are you?'

'No, I don't have to be.'

'Well, I'll see you tomorrow.'

'Jack, don't hang up.'

'I have to. I'm going to wake everyone up. I'm just standing here in the hallway. I'll see you at lunch, okay?'

This morning I woke up with the phone in my hand and felt like a fool.

Patricia seemed glad to see me but asked several times if I am all right, said I've lost weight and look a little 'hollow.' Summer semester brings freshmen admitted on probation. What a day of children. I had to argue about the difference between the Library of Congress and Dewey decimal system for ten minutes to a young girl. She couldn't understand why history was downstairs and the fiction upstairs . . .

Finally, she just asked me if I could find Emily Dickinson for her. I pointed out the card catalog to her, but she'd never used anything except microfiche machines in her public library, so she didn't understand the cards in the drawers. Then she broke her beads, twisting and twisting them. I thought *I* would turn blue before they exploded off her chest. We crawled around picking them up and I realized that she was interested in me. I laughed, which made her blush, because she was so green she knew it and thought she'd missed the joke somehow.

A kid brought two copies of the same book to the desk for check-out. It had regular binding on one, library binding on another, probably because someone's dog chewed the cover off it. He insisted on checking them both out because 'there aren't very many books on that subject.'

There was a student who thought I was a foreigner when I spoke, and began to speak very slowly and condescendingly to me. Then, when I pointed out that she was wrong in looking for something (a miscopied call number), she became frustrated, thinking that I didn't understand her. I told her to stand still and I got the book for her. She was quiet after that as I stamped her books.

Patricia came by and asked me when I would like to go to lunch. I tried to tell her that I didn't care – whenever. I didn't feel much like playing her game. She seemed to understand, and for the first time since I've worked for her, she told me when to go. It was all right for Ornette, who is back for the summer. I think she and her boyfriend are getting along better.

After she had gone, I picked up the phone and dialed Jack's extension. I looked around to make sure there were no oncoming students with books in hand.

Someone answered, 'Psychology department.'

'May I speak to Jack Berdo?'

'One moment.'

Jack came on the phone. 'Hello?'

'Would you have lunch with me at one?'

'Certainly. And I have your mail, too.'

'My mail?' I didn't like the sound of that.

'I got my grades this morning,' she said. 'So I dropped by your place on the way to work and got yours, too. Thought I would bring them to you, but I was running late.'

What did I get in chemistry?'

There was a sound of paper tearing. 'A "C".'

'Thank God.'

'The rest are "Bs." I thought you would do better than that in English history.'

'Been a tough semester. I was distracted.'

'Well, I have to go and ask Ben some questions and he's off the phone now. I'll see you at one. Come up to the office.'

'Meet halfway?'

'Well, I was thinking that we could go to the Pantry and it's far enough that we should go in the truck. I'm parked right outside the building.'

'Okay, meet you at the truck.'

'No, come up to room 308,' she said, 'I'll see you later.'

At one, I stood outside the door of the Social Science building. I had worn warm clothes because of the way the morning had looked, but going inside the building was a cool relief. From every few doors came a droning lecture. I walked up the stairs slowly, feeling dread of room 308.

The secretary was gone. I stood in the office and looked into the doors I could see from the desk, but saw no one I recognized. I didn't really want to explore. A lot of doors were closed. I felt that Jack and Miller were nearby, but Jack wasn't waiting. She was busy. So I read the departmental bulletin board. Interesting to compare the psychology department with history – there were notices for volunteer work, some non-professional job openings and such. In the history department, we see no job notices – only graduate schools and fellowships abroad.

One of the professors came out of his office and peered at me. 'May I help you?' he asked suspiciously.

'No, I'm waiting for someone.'

He shrugged and got some water, then returned to his office.

I sensed Jack. I walked toward the bend of the L-shaped corridor beyond the front office. 'Jack?' I called.

'Kolya, is that you?' she said.

I stopped in the hallway. I didn't know that she and Miller were in the same office without at least a partition between them. He stood at a filing cabinet and nodded at me slightly. She sat beside, not at, the only desk in the office, her hand resting lightly on the keyboard of a desk calculator. She smiled at me. 'Hi,' she said and her voice sounded a little shy.

'Hi,' I replied. 'Ready?'

'You've met Ben?' she asked.

Ben, is it, I thought? But I knew there was nothing to be jealous about between them. She admired him. I reluctantly looked at him and he nodded again.

'Good afternoon,' he said in my language.

I stared at him, knowing what it was he was trying to do.

'Jack says you understand Russian,' he said. 'Don't you?'

Oh, you're a clever man, I thought, but I felt nothing malicious coming from him, as much as I tried. He is too clever even for that. Not only does he know everything about me somehow, but he knows how to mask himself. Of course, he's a great deal more intellect than emotion, and I certainly would have a headful if I could read *minds* like they do in the books, but things don't work that way.

'Yes, I do,' I said to him.

'I was wondering if you would consider doing a service for some friends of mine.' His words were flawless, his accent good, but he sounded formal as people often do in a foreign language that they know well.

He seemed completely at ease, not as if he were about to spring anything big or awful on me. He also seemed to regard me with that curiosity that's always been part of his 'scent.'

He continued. 'I do some interpreting for Soviet Jews that have recently arrived in the country. At home, there are many interpreters, but here I have discovered that there is a shortage. I've talked to some agencies and they say there aren't enough to help, especially volunteers in the institutions in Denver.' The name of the city sounded foreign from his mouth. 'Would you consider helping out?'

'I don't think I can. I visit Denver only occasionally.'

'You have family in the city?' he asked.

'I don't drive,' I said. 'I suppose I could help over the phone.' I was feeling sand shift under my feet. Not only that, but I felt a change in Miller's mood. He was treading carefully.

'That would help,' he said. 'Do you speak Lithuanian or Polish?'

I felt a prickling of ancestral insult (something my grandmother had given to me without my father's consent). 'No.' But then I realized that he was trying to fit my background into Russia, which was another clue to match me with what he knew. 'I'll give you my phone number,' I said, and I waited as he took out a small notebook from his breast pocket and uncapped his pen. I shook my head, then looked at Jack. 'What's my telephone number?'

'You talking to me? What did you say?'

'What's my phone number?' I asked her in English.

She recited it and I watched Miller write it down. He guarded his page. It was probably filled with notes about me, about my father and grandfather. It was probably on a page marked D. I felt that Miller was uneasy.

'How did you know that I speak Russian?' I asked as conversationally as I could.

Miller looked at Jack, then back at me. I understood that as the answer. Then he smiled, 'I asked Jack about your . . . ' For the first time, he seemed to be searching for a word. ' . . . manner. You remember that we met at her house.' He put his notebook away.

'Yes.'

'In fact, I was interested because I am interested in Russians, Jewish or not. I thought I recognized your . . . uh, manner.' The word still didn't suit him but he couldn't think of a replacement. 'I'd like to talk to you sometime about your background.'

'I am from Denver, Colorado. I am not a Russian,' I said. 'I am an American.'

Dr Miller laughed. 'I didn't mean to say . . . well, maybe you could tell me about your family sometime, then?'

I gave a sort of nod that I thought might mean, I'm being polite, acknowledging your words, but not saying yes. That would have been enough for most people to realize that I had no interest in what they wanted of me. But, no, this man is a hunter.

'Perhaps you and Jack could come over sometime and have dinner. My wife will be joining me soon, but it's lonely for me until she gets here.' He said this in English and Jack sat up with interest at the invitation.

'Perhaps,' I said at last. 'We'd better go, Jack, I only have forty-five minutes of my lunch hour left now.'

'What about this weekend?' Miller asked quickly, looking toward Jack.

'We don't have any plans, do we?' Jack asked.

I couldn't think fast enough. Dinner in his apartment. I suffocated already after three minutes' conversation. How could I do it? I felt my child's self rising up, screaming 'No, no!' but the socialized adult was silent, thinking politically of Jack. I tried to think of a soft no.

'We'd love to,' Jack said. 'I'll talk to you about it when I get back. I think Kolya's hungry, his eyes are getting

166

glassy.' She laughed and took my hand.

We walked down the corridor together. I was so angry with her, angry with myself for being mute while she sentenced me to an evening with a psychologist, that I was stiff-legged.

'Hey,' she said, 'what's the matter with you? Are you mad at me because I didn't come over last night?'

'No.'

'Oh, no nothing's wrong,' she said, mocking me. 'C'mon, what's the matter?' She squeezed my hand.

Isn't she in it with him? How can I go on fooling myself about this? This whole spring has been an elaborate pursuit, but how could they know that I would fall in love with her? They could have planned this right from the beginning, and here I am, holding her hand and going along with it. What a fool. I let go of her hand, trying to remember how much I had told her about myself over these months.

All I know for certain is that Susanne is real, unplanned and Susanne is dying.

I wanted to talk to her.

But I couldn't ask *her* questions. Suppose it wasn't so, and Susanne would think that I was crazy, or paranoid or something, if I asked her about the plot that Jack and Dr Miller had cooked up. I'll just keep quiet. I'll keep quiet around everyone. I won't say anything that I wouldn't say to Miller. I'll break off with her perhaps. She doesn't care for me anyway.

We didn't speak much through our meal, which was fine with me. But Jack acted edgy. She asked me why I'd called her in the middle of the night. I apologized and said I would never do it again.

Goddamn mind-rapers, that's what they are. And I'm supposed to be civil and get through, get through no matter how I feel. I'm sick of it.

We didn't make any plans to see each other after work, so I left a few minutes early and walked over to my old liquor store. That clerk doesn't work there any more. He probably is working on a Harvard law degree now. I bought a bottle and went to the park and drank my booze out of a paper bag.

Talked to a resident of the park. He's only thirty, but doesn't have his front teeth and has lived everywhere from New Jersey to California, usually on the streets, in Salvation Armies. I think he has *pozhar-golava*, too. I asked him, but he said no, and pretended to be too drunk to understand me. But he seemed to understand me more than anyone I've met for a long time, other than Susanne. He told me that he spends every summer in Colorado and in the winter he goes to Austin, Texas. He told me about a place called the drag where college girls wear shorts all year around.

It can happen to anyone, but I forgot that I'd moved and tried to get back into my old apartment. It was a little embarrassing to try the keys in the lock and have someone else open the door. He was scared shitless of me, then I remembered that I didn't live there.

I walked to Gus's and Gus put me up on his sofa, just like the old days.

1 June

Susanne asked me to come over. She said she was calling for Jack because Jack thought I wouldn't come if she asked. Why are you angry with Jack, she asked? I'm not, I said, I'll be right over.

I drank a lot and got on my bicycle and rode over to the Berdos' for dinner. When I first got there, no one seemed to be at home. I opened the front door and walked in. Heard voices in the back yard. Julie was answering to something Jack had just said. I put my bottle of wine in the refrigerator.

'Kolya?'

Susanne met me in the dining room. I hadn't seen her for about five days. She wasn't wearing a scarf, her hair was patchy but seemed to be growing back a bit. Her skin was ginger, which made the little hairs more silver by contrast. The brown color of her eyes washed into the white. She was as beautiful as some alien being.

I put my arms out to her and held her. I felt the chill take hold of me. 'Susanne.'

We retreated from the voices just beyond the screen door, back into the living room. I thought for a moment that she was going to take me upstairs, but we stopped on the carpeted stairway and sat down there, thigh to thigh.

'Why aren't you and Jack getting along?'

'I don't know,' I said, staring at her. 'God, you're beautiful. Look at the color of your skin.'

She laughed. 'How strange that you should say that. I almost believe you, too.'

I smiled at her. I took her hand and wrapped it in my own large hand and rested it on my knee.

'I don't think I'm going to last much longer.'

'You look fine.'

'No, I don't mean that. I think I've come to my end, the me inside here. Soon the body will be lying in bed all day long getting bedsores and vomiting. *I* won't last that long.'

'Susanne, you shouldn't look at it so bleakly.'

I felt it, however. I could almost see the finish, too. I wanted it, it was so easy. Easier than the fight to stay.

'The other morning I came down . . . ' She pointed toward the living room and we both looked over to the sofa and chairs. 'Paul was listening to a song that was "our song." You know, it was popular on the radio when we fell in love. And he just sat there, smoking a cigarette, which he hasn't done for years. But I stood there,' she said, pointing to the floor at our feet, the end of the stairway. 'He never saw or heard me. He was thinking about a Susanne that lived a long time ago. She doesn't exist any more, so why should I go on with this?'

'I wish I could do something for you,' I said. I loved her as I've never loved anyone else in my life.

'You have. You've listened to me, you've held me.

You're the only one who doesn't look through me.' She kissed my pink hand with her jaundiced lips.

'The doctor ordered some pills for me when I was getting better, in the hospital. Mood elevators, he called them. I bit my nails. I cried and wanted to scream. So I stood on my bed and screamed and screamed. Caused quite a scene. The nurses came and pulled me down and baby-talked me. They didn't want me to hurt myself, they said.' She laughed, covering her mouth with her hand, as if she'd told a naughty secret. 'Dr Goldman came and said he'd talked it over with another doctor and they wanted to give me a drug that would make me feel sick, but might give me a few more months. Oh, Kolya, a few more months!' She laughed.

I laughed with her. I knew the surprise that anyone could think of offering her more time, when the strongest urge was to move into that place, that existence that wipes out the fear.

She kissed me quite suddenly, and I held her hand and touched the back of her neck.

'Susanne, take me with you.'

She just looked at me. Then said, 'If I could be Jack, I would want to live. You would make me want to live.'

For a moment, I wanted her to turn pink, be happy, grow old, I wanted her to be with me. And me with her.

She's *leaving* me, I thought.

'Is that for me?' she asked, and her fingertip touched my cheek. 'A tear for me?'

I heard Jack's voice coming into the kitchen and I wanted to get away. Susanne stood, too, apprehensively. I took the stairs two at a time and shut myself in the bathroom. It smelled so soapy, the towels were thick, the toilet paper like velvet, the carpet and shower curtains in brilliant blues and oranges. I rinsed my face with cold water and peered in the mirror. I looked awful. I looked like someone else, someone much older than Nicholas Alexandrovich. Maybe I should go to Grandmama's tomorrow, I thought. Susanne, Susanne, how I'm hurting. Need a drink. Tomorrow we're supposed to go to Miller's. Have to do that, get it out of the way. Maybe it's time to run. Susanne, oh, God, she's going to die. Shit. Susanne. Jesus Christ, I look awful.

'Kolya?'

'Just a minute.'

'Are you all right?'

'Please, Susanne, just a minute.' I sat down on the carpeted toilet seat. I couldn't move, I was so tired.

'Are you drunk?'

I took a deep breath and opened the door. 'Oh,' I said, and knowing that it was badly said, made it worse by saying, 'I thought you were Su – your mother.'

'It's going to be one of those nights, isn't it?' Jack said. She sounded sad. 'You're going to drink too much, things are going to get in our way, everything will be just too much for you to handle.'

'Jack, don't do this to me. I'll try.' I wanted to stay. I wanted to look at Susanne. I tried to smile, but it didn't seem to work.

'How could you possibly think I was my mother? We don't sound alike.'

'I'm sorry,' I said. I felt like weeping again.

She stared at the floor. 'Maybe you should just go. Mom's been picking at us all day. We're all like this. Maybe you'd be better off at home tonight.'

'All right,' I said, agreeing with her. 'Let me get my wine.' She squeezed up against the wall as I passed her and headed down the stairs. I stopped in the dining room.

Trouble.

Paul's voice rose above a clatter of dishes. 'Stop it, Suz, stop it!'

'And then you buried her because you'd never asked her anything about what she wanted done. She wanted to be cremated.' Susanne's voice was louder than usual, but flat and detached. 'And you buried her in a horrible green dress even though her skin was the color of a pumpkin.'

'Shut up!'

'I heard that you never even cried when she died because

171

it was such a shock to you. I wanted to tell you that your wife was dying, but you wouldn't listen to me.'

A tremendous shattering noise shot through me. I don't know if it was my nerves or something breaking in the kitchen. Jack put her hand on my arm. 'Please go home, Kolya.'

'We have company, Paul, don't throw things.' Susanne came out into the dining room with a little smile. 'Please excuse him. His wife has died and he's gone a little crazy.'

I felt all the agony in Paul's cry. It stuck in my mind and wouldn't let go. Jarred all my wires with disharmonic frequencies.

And the world burst into flames. I felt it right through me – hissing and snapping, pulling me to pieces, and when Jack tried to speak to me her voice was melted, her face on fire.

I headed for the door.

'Are you hot?' Mikhail asked me. 'Take a swim.'

Then I was somewhere else. Leaves blew over dry sticks and dust on the ground, the air smelled like snow. I shoved my hands into my jeans pockets and looked up into a dying sky.

The whole world is dying. The flames are flickering out. The stars are fading, the sun is steaming. The cells in my body wither with every step I take with every breath I breathe with every thought I think with every feeling I steal from you.

There were voices. And cold water dribbling on my forehead, then a feel of wet terry cloth on my forehead.

'Papa?' I asked, but I couldn't see for the orange light. 'What can I do now? I'm stuck here.'

'I wish he would speak English. Kolya, talk to me in English, I can't understand you.'

'I can't remember,' I said because I couldn't make my mouth form the words. The words of others, their language.

'Julie, don't you remember any Russian? Don't you have a dictionary?'

'It's too fast!'

Dr Wall was in my bedroom when I woke up. He sat on the mattress with his notepad on his knee. 'Now, Nick, I'm not the kind of doctor who gives you shots or takes your temperature. You can just talk to me about things that bother you.'

'I'm not Nick.'

'Oh. What do you want me to call you?'

'Nicholas.'

'All right, Nicholas.' And he reached down on the floor beside my bed. He'd brought his brass elephant with the hollowed-out back. He exchanged the pen he'd been using for another, probably because I'd told him a different name.

What's bothering you, Nicholas?

I have sex with my parents. My father tries to shut me out, but he can't hide me from Miranda. She's afraid of me and she's left the house. I don't even have to leave my bedroom to share their bed. If I'm asleep, I wake up and make the bed wet.

'Kolya?'

'You can't lie to me. I know. I know what's going on. I know when you're lying to me, you dirty bastard, so get out of my room. I've been through with you for years. Forget what I said.'

'Kolya, listen to me. The fire's gone now. But would you like a drink just to make sure?'

'Don't give him anything to drink.'

'He needs it,' Miller said. 'Go on, Jack, you aren't helping.'

I sat up. Miller handed me a glass of wine. 'I take it black,' I said, and drank the wine.

'We need to call your father, don't we?'

'Yes,' I said. 'No.' He didn't need to be involved in this. 'Yes.' I wanted him. I told Miller his phone number.

That is the way I remember it happening, but when I look it over I know that some of that is a little confused. When I woke up again, my father was sitting on the floor, his head leaning against the wall. A slight snore came from his open mouth.

'Papa, what are you doing here?' I asked. The sun was so bright.

'They said you were asking for me,' Papa said, lifting his head and looking at me blearily. 'Are you all right?'

I felt strange – cottony and numb. 'I'm drugged, aren't I?'

'I think you might be. It feels to me that you are. He's a psychiatrist. They have little black bags.' He smiled. 'I'm glad you're all right, now, though.'

'I don't like being drugged,' I complained.

'No, I don't imagine it's very comfortable.' He paused, then said, 'I talked to him.'

'Him? Who?'

'Dr Miller.'

'What do you mean you talked to him?'

'I didn't tell him anything, Kolya.' He eased himself up from the floor arthritically and came over to sit beside me on the mattress. 'But I knew that he knew, and he knew I knew.' He laughed. 'It's all a game, just trying not to say it. But he isn't a bad man, I rather like him.'

I tried to sit up but my head was too heavy. The popping in my eyes was frequent.

'What happened?' Papa asked.

'You wouldn't believe it. It was the scream of recognition. I just happened to be there when Paul was hit with everything Susanne has, and he had a fire in his head, too. Jesus!'

'Death,' he said.

'Susanne's not . . . ?' I asked suddenly.

'Oh, no, no, Kolya,' he said, reassuring me. 'I talked to her last night on the telephone.'

'I don't like being drugged,' I said. I needed to get out of bed and pee, but my body was sluggish.

'Kolya, I need to ask you something before you move away from me.' He misunderstood my feeling of urgency. 'Please stay away from the family until it's over.'

'Papa,' I said, 'I can't leave Susanne now, can I?'

'What about Jack?'

'Jack? She's trapped me. I fell for it all.'

'Trapped you? What do you mean? Is she pregnant?'

'No. This – Miller.'

'Oh, you're mistaken. I spent all night sitting with Jack watching you breathe, Kolya. She has no idea what's going on. She thinks you're having delirium tremens and she's a little disgusted with you for being an alcoholic.'

'But!' I was amazed.

'Miller hasn't told her anything. You haven't told her anything. What do you think it looks like?' Papa sighed. 'I like Jack. She's afraid of you, though. She's terrified. I don't think she's going to love you any longer. She's stuck by you as a loyal friend.'

I felt an ache at those words.

'Dr Miller is a good man, Kolya. He feels guilty about using us, but something important is drawing him to us. He needs us somehow. Have you felt that?'

'I suppose so. He needs us for a research paper,' I said. 'No matter that he ruins our lives.'

'Would it?'

I looked at my father. I wished that I could read him, but I was too numb, too drugged, and my bladder was the most urgent thing on my mind, in spite of the importance of the conversation. 'What do you mean?' I asked.

'Do you remember,' he said, as if it were the beginning of a long story, 'the night I picked you up from the Litvaks' house? We talked to you for a little while about how you are different from others, and this is the way your life would be. It is harder in America, there is more pressure to be like others here. These days they even have classes and workshops in how to be like others – well adjusted. Well, after you went to bed that night, we all talked about the difference between you and the rest of the family. You needed more help than we ever did, but you got the wrong kind of help. There are doctors unlike Dr Wall. He was a mistake, the hospital was a bigger mistake, but I couldn't fight it. Especially with you having seizures every night. I couldn't even get you into a private room. They were afraid you'd do violence to yourself. The school was a mistake.'

My father lifted his hands up to an invisible power to appeal and apologize. 'I have failed in so many ways to do what is right for you, and sometimes it was out of my hands, but not always. I have made great, great mistakes.' His eyes filled.

'Papa,' I said.

'But, I don't care what they know or don't know about me any more. I will tell everything about the Dals, if someone has to hear it. Grandmama can't be hurt by it. The only one to suffer is you. And *that's* what hurts me.' He wiped his eyes and was quiet for a long time.

I looked away from him.

'I've always been tormented by the fact that your life has been hell, Kolya,' he said.

I shut my eyes. I sank back into the bed.

'If I see a way to help you, will you believe me that it isn't another plot to rip you to pieces? Will you believe *me*?' he asked. I could feel him looking at me.

'I will believe your intentions are good,' I said.

'Then do you give me permission to talk to Dr Miller on the condition that he leaves you alone?'

I said nothing.

'In return, I want you to stay away from Susanne, from the family, and only see Jack away from them.'

I thought about it. 'I can't say yes, Papa. I can't say that I won't see Susanne.'

He sighed. He put his hands on his knees and said nothing. I struggled out of bed and went to the toilet at last.

I am remembering things from much later, not having had a chance to sit at my desk and write until now.

A few days after I went to the Berdos' I slept a lot, and Jack stayed with me the whole day. She fed me, sat beside me on the bed and read. She said that she'd cancelled our dinner with Dr Miller.

In the late afternoon, we took a couple of chairs outside and sat on the lawn. It was hot, but in a pleasant way. I tried to apologize to her and tell her that I thought things would be better from now on. And I really believed it at the time, but Jack only budged a little. She didn't really seem to think anything would change – how could I blame her? She would just have to see for herself.

We sat through dusk. I love dusk, when all the birds begin their tremendous rackets and swarm from tree to tree. Lights go on inside houses, children follow the lights; everything settles down.

Jack sat in the rocking chair. She was still wearing shorts and a little top, which had been good for sunning hours ago, but now I could see that the evening breeze was giving her goosebumps. I also noticed that the grass needed watering, the ground was dry and lumpy. I wasn't being the tenant I'd promised to be. So I helped Jack carry the chairs back inside, set the water sprinklers with a lot of domestic satisfaction, and turned on the radio.

Jack had pulled on a T-shirt. With her hand on her forehead, she looked as if she had a headache. I asked her. 'No, just thinking.'

'About?' I asked.

'I was wishing I could go somewhere far, far away,' she said.

I felt heavy. It was all going wrong, and I was to blame. Jack is going to leave me. The first woman I had ever thought I could actually stay with and it was all going wrong. 'You could, I suppose,' I said.

'It might be too late next year, or I'll feel obligated to

spend my money elsewhere. But I can't go now.' Her voice was soft.

I sat down at my desk, sorting papers. Needed to do something. 'I don't suppose you'd miss me at all,' I said, feeling nasty, and also wanting a reaction.

She looked over at me, then held out her hand. 'I don't think you have any idea how I feel right now.'

I couldn't help but smile at that. Actually, it was true. Right at that moment, I didn't. I was as confused as Jack. I took her hand, scooting a little closer to her chair.

'I just want to get away from *everything*,' she went on. 'I'm so tired.'

'Yes,' I said. 'Everything includes me.'

'Stop, Kolya.'

'You would probably rather go to Italy now because I couldn't go to Miller's for supper.'

'I know you're not feeling well,' she said, looking away from me. 'Maybe I should go home now.'

'Stay a little longer.'

'I'm depressed,' she said.

'I am, too. Everyone's depressed. I imagine even your Dr Miller is depressed. He probably doesn't have much of a social life here in town.'

'He's not *my* Dr Miller. I wish you wouldn't say that. It bothers me.' She withdrew her hand from mine.

'I don't want him to come at me with his needles ever again,' I said. 'That's why I feel so rotten. It's worse than a hangover, damned drugs.' I wished that we could start all over again, but I was miserable and wanted to tell her so. I felt that somehow she was to blame.

'You're lucky he came last night, Kolya,' she said, bitterly. 'I really didn't know what to do with you, but he got you out of my house, took care of you here, and wouldn't let your father pay him anything. I know you hate psychiatrists in general, but I don't think you should feel that way about Ben.'

'I . . . ' At that moment, I realized that Jack was making me angry. She was angry, I was not. Not really. I was too

178

stupefied to feel that much about anything, but she was spilling over into me. I needed a drink.

'I wish everyone would just leave me alone!' She sat very still with tears silently, steadily, tracking down her face.

'Jack,' I said, and moved toward her, but she put her hand up, motioning me away.

I got up and got a drink, poured myself a small glass, and poured Jack a little glass of wine. As I handed it to her, I felt someone coming. It was Miller. He was *not* depressed, and in fact seemed in a friendly mood.

The doorbell rang. Jack wiped her eyes and looked at me.

'I love you,' I said. I had a sudden feeling that it could be my last chance to tell her. I touched her hair. She was so distant from me that I wanted to call out her name. I answered the door.

Benjamin Miller stood at the door with two white paper bags. 'Am I intruding?' he asked.

Yes.

'No,' Jack said. 'What's all this? Chinese food!' Jack seemed recovered from her depression suddenly at the prospect of egg rolls and sweet-and-sour.

'Hi, Kolya, feeling better?' he asked.

'I'm fine.'

'I brought some tea, too. Would you like me to fix it with the food? Have you eaten? Are you sure I'm not intruding?' Miller headed for the kitchen and started to unpack.

Jack followed him. She said, 'Yes, no, yes.'

They laughed together. I could see that it was a joke between them. They took over my kitchen, getting down plates, boiling water, finding the tea strainer, chattering about the restaurant the food had come from, about the food itself – 'Oh, look at these, they're beautiful!'

I went into the bedroom to search for my cigarettes. I found them and sat on the bed to light one up and stayed there, just sitting and smoking. I didn't want to go out into my own kitchen. I was trapped here, invaded. Thought about going out the window, but Jack peeked in.

'Don't you want to eat?' she asked. She questioned more than that with her expression.

'Yes, just a moment and I'll be there.'

She returned to the kitchen. Through the wall, I could hear them talking in more subdued voices. About me. How is he now, he's okay but surly, etc. I imagined the conversation. Waited until it took a more natural turn and they began to oo and ah over the food again, clattering plates onto the table. I hate walking into conversations about me and having everything go dead.

Miller looked up at me when I came into the kitchen. He was wearing jeans and his sleeves were rolled up. He looked younger and more casual than I'd ever seen him. He looked away because there was nothing we could say to each other to break the tension right then.

'This is great.' Jack sat down at the table and looked happily into the white cartons. 'I didn't realize how hungry I was. C'mon, Kolya.'

I took a spoon of everything and sat down at the table with them.

'I was sorry that you couldn't make it for dinner at my place. Hope you don't mind the presumption.' Miller looked at me again.

I shrugged. 'This is good,' I said. 'I think Jack was about to leave anyway, since all I have here is peanut butter and beets.'

'Was I?' She looked surprised.

Ben – somehow I was thinking of him as Ben, too, because he sat there in faded jeans eating with his fingers – grinned. 'To be honest, I'm a little lonely without my wife and kids. After seventeen years, you get used to noise, waiting for the bathroom, eating at the same time of day, hungry or not. I don't know what I'd do without them. This life is too quiet.'

'Isn't your wife coming soon?' Jack asked.

'As soon as Rachel gets into summer camp.'

'How old are your children?' I knew that it was a question one should ask of people discussing their children.

'Michael's fifteen, Rachel's eleven. Michael is at school this summer. I can't keep him from studying, even in the summer.'

'Fifteen,' Jack said. 'You don't seem old enough to have a son that old.'

'My dear, I am forty,' he said, and laughed. 'That's given me plenty of time to have children growing up.'

I ate without appetite. The drugs that this man injected into my body were still affecting me, but I also felt suffocated by his presence. He was so *aware* of me. I could feel him watching me without looking, listening to me though I said little or nothing, waiting for me to give him something, somehow.

'Jack, would you please open the window?' I asked.

She looked at me, and I was about to get the reply that she would have given her little sister, but she got up and cranked the window open.

'Thank you,' I said.

They dug in for seconds as I made my way through the first plateful. I tried to think of things conversational; I'm not made for conversation. I felt dull. Why would anyone choose to be around me, I wondered? What on earth did Jack ever see in me? I was caught looking at her with that in mind.

They were reading my feelings, I think, for there was a pause.

Then the chatter continued between Ben and Jack. It seemed as if they must talk very little about themselves at work because they were discovering things that other co-workers might already know.

'People are so nervous when they find out I'm a psychiatrist,' Ben said. 'But I'm a teacher. I barely got through my residency. I was terrible at telling people how to fix themselves. Me, the klutz, telling them how to run their lives. I was more interested in the organic side of it.'

Jack laughed.

Klutz, I thought. He's conning us.

'I like teaching, I like research. Those patients drove me

nuts, but the field is interesting from an academic stand-point.'

I tried not to smile. Dammit. He was a likeable and admirable man, this Benjamin Miller, umbrella man. He was tolerant, intelligent, generous, and had a sort of naive air sometimes. He wanted us to like him, too, and all the bit with the Chinese food was real. He was disappointed not to have us over for dinner. Believe me, I know when someone lies.

I almost thought, sitting there, listening to him prattle so charmingly, and grunting out a sentence or two every now and then when he pulled one out of me, that he might just be a psychiatrist in town, employing Jack by chance.

But no, there is always a little something else there. Not necessarily sinister, but a quest.

I am the holy grail. I am what he seeks. And there were times that I guessed this by a gesture, a word, a look. He hinted to me every now and then.

Then the guessing stopped.

Jack got up to go to the bathroom. Ben got up and poured each of us more tea, and we sat there with our elbows amidst ruins of fried rice and brown gravy, the bottle of Kikkoman still uncapped, the lids of the white cartons standing. It no longer smelled good, I was too full of food. I hardly wanted to move. The tea felt pleasant going down, washing out a path.

There was silence. I lit a cigarette, not looking at Miller. It was like a silence between people who care about each other, and I was nervous of it.

'I want to talk to you,' he said in Russian.

'Oh?' I tapped my cigarette into a gooey carton.

'Yes.' Once again, I noticed how formal Ben's speech is in Russian. 'I don't know how to approach this. I do know that you don't want to talk about it, but I can make this promise: no one, not even Jack, has to know what we talk about. But I think you should be honest with her. She needs to know. She has a low opinion of you right now, which is undeserved.'

'What are you talking about?'

Ben faltered. I sensed that he'd held off the direct approach because he still wasn't positive, and he seemed to know that hope could have tainted all he had guessed so far.

'Research?' I asked him, prodding, acting interested and uninitiated.

'Yes, research,' he said blandly.

I was surprised at how calm I remained. Only felt a little strange in my hands and head, but my stomach was steady, happily stuffed with supper. Here was the moment. The umbrella man as grand inquisitor, and I sat digesting egg roll. I had very little alcohol in me. I had never thought it would be like that. I had imagined something much more dramatic than this 40-year-old schoolteacher wiping his hands on a paper towel and actually acting a little nervous of *me*.

'On what?' I asked.

'Russian immigrants. A particular family of Russian immigrants.'

'Oh, I see. Well, I'm an American, but I suppose I might have some connections.'

'I am talking about *pozhar-golava*,' he said.

'What's that?' I admit that I did think about getting up for a drink then, but I smoked my cigarette as actively as I could instead.

Jack came back into the kitchen. She sat down and sighed as if very tired and made no attempt to jump into the conversation. She heard the Russian, and looked at her fingernails.

'It's a sensitivity to other people's feelings, an acute awareness of others.' He had to search for a word or two, but nonetheless, he said it all dramatically.

'I am wondering what this has to do with Russians,' I said.

'You honestly don't know what I'm talking about?' Ben asked. He looked at me with hope in his face.

'No.'

He sat back, looked over at Jack, who was staring at the

floor. I felt depressed just looking at her. Jack was only staying because she didn't want to go home, either. I wanted to touch her face and make her smile, but I had as much reserve about it as if I barely knew her.

'We're being rude,' Ben said, but then asked, still in Russian, 'You wouldn't mind if I told a story about the family of Russians that I am researching then? You may remember things that you haven't heard of for years. Jack may find it an interesting story, too.'

'I'd like to hear about Russians,' I said. I drank down my tea and lit another cigarette with the first.

'I was telling Kolya about some of the things I've heard from immigrants,' Ben explained to Jack. Jack turned toward us again. Ben looked at me. He was asking me if he should go through with it, but I made my face a mask. 'One of the strangest is a tale that my training made me disbelieve entirely when I first heard it. But the second time, I started to wonder. Then I met someone involved first hand.'

First hand? I felt as if I'd been prodded with a sharp stick. Who could that be? Who could have been left?

I had a moment of panic, seeing Mikhail rising out of the lake. Ah, but he couldn't have.

Jack leaned forward, interested.

Ben warmed up. 'In the farmlands, there was once a family which had a knack, you might call it, for knowing what a person felt. A sort of psychic link, if you will, as if that person experienced the same feelings – not thoughts – as the others that they were near, or cared about.'

I reached for Jack's hand. She took mine, but never looked away from Ben as he told the story. All about the family that had been that way for generations beyond memory, the ability passing through all direct descendants but the females were only carriers. No one bothered the family in their community. They were accepted and left alone, and they even intermarried with other families. They were respected, hard-working, close-knit.

Then as the family grew and prospered, they crowded their living quarters more and more. At the turn of the century, and into that first decade or so, one of the two brothers had produced an especially large number of sons. Sometime in the 1920s, this house held a grandmother, the two brothers and their wives, their children, some of whom had their own children, too.

The grandmother lay dying upstairs.

This, with the crowded conditions, was difficult for them all to cope with well, but one of the grown, but unmarried, grandsons started to go mad.

He said there was fire in his head, fire everywhere.

I got up to get a drink. I couldn't sit quietly. I didn't want to feel it when Jack realized what was up. I poured a little vodka in my teacup.

Ben talked on. The mad brother finally broke down completely one night. He went from room to room, stabbing and killing his own family. He was quiet, apparently, because it wasn't until he got to his brother Fyodor's room that anyone tried to stop him. His brother was ready, though, the messages of the dying had reached him.

He saved himself, his wife, and his young son by convincing his brother that the fire would go out if he swam in the lake, that it would clean the blood and quench the fire. The mad brother went into the lake and never came out.

Ben held out his hands as if the story had run through his fingers.

Jack wrinkled her nose. 'Depressing. Sounds like an old folk tale, doesn't it?'

I hated both of them.

I drank, then got another drink. I didn't care what Jack thought as I opened the cupboard. It was too late. There was nothing to salvage from all this, except for me to get away.

'And then the people in the community turned against the survivors. The man had lost his whole family, and the neighbors came and burned the house down.'

'Interesting,' Jack said, 'how in that country they would attribute strange behavior to something supernatural. Here we'd be taking buccal smears to check for defective chromosomes. It's like the stories of people who supposedly have haunted houses, but it just turns out that they are a little different from other people. It's like believing in ghosts . . . ' She stopped suddenly, and a look crossed her face that I could not read. I didn't know what she was feeling, I couldn't guess. I was lost.

Ben watched me.

'Those people,' Jack said, suddenly. 'Is this true, did you say?'

'So far as I can tell,' Ben said softly. 'I've talked to people who've met them, or knew of the story.'

'And then what?'

I got up and stood at the kitchen door, looking out at the street lights beyond my landlord's house. How blue they were, how nice the evening was, so cool . . .

Ben spoke, still trying to reach me. 'The problem is, though, that the surviving family has taken on the guilt of the brother. They've damned themselves.'

'You really believe this stuff?' Jack asked, incredulously.

I turned and looked at her.

She has no idea. She has made no connections. She hears a tale of faraway people in fairyland trouble, and she has not the slightest conception of the madness that has brushed her own lips and breasts and thighs for all these nights since I found her.

Poor Jack.

I pitied her because she seemed such a fool, the only one not to get the joke. And it was unlike her, she was sharp, discerning, at least about *things*. Maybe not about people. She doesn't understand the motivations that lie darkly in others' hearts; she doesn't have that vision. She's an innocent, no matter how wise she becomes. I pitied her, and I also knew that I would never love her in the same way again, nor would she love me. The gulf was too wide. She lives in a world of balanced accounts and reason, and I am lost and lonely in that world.

I raised my glass a little to toast her journeys far away

from me; Ben saw it, and he saw, I think, the tears that had come to my eyes.

'Yes,' Ben said. He had a sad look. 'I can't tell you more than that, though.'

Jack stared at the floor thoughtfully.

'And now what?' I asked him in Russian.

He just looked at me. 'I can help you, but I just want to talk to you, that's all.'

'I am fine. I don't need help.'

Ben stood. 'I just remembered that Katherine is going to call me this evening. I think I'd better go now.'

Jack stood. 'I should be going, too,' she said, stretching her arms. 'I'll help you clean up, if you like, Kolya.'

'No, it's all right.' We all moved into the living room and stood by the door. Jack looked around as if she'd forgotten something, but she seemed to see nothing. I think she was disillusioned about Ben because he believed such a tale.

Ben extended his hand to me. 'Good night, Kolya, and thank you for your hospitality.'

'Of course,' I said, feeling empty. I didn't care if they stayed or left. I didn't even care if Dr Benjamin Miller took Jack home and made love to her all night. I didn't care if he sat and talked to me all night about everything he knew. I didn't care. It just didn't matter.

Ben left and we watched him get into his car.

'Well,' she said.

'Yes, well.'

She patted my back. 'Take care, Kolya, I'll see you later.'

We made a short, amicable good-night kiss and then I watched her get into her truck.

I sat in the kitchen amidst the soggy cartons, smoking and drinking until Susanne arrived.

14 June

He asks me why I can't write about it. He sees me sitting motionless with my pen for half an hour. I can't recount this, I said. He said, I won't read it, but I think you should write it down because that's the only way you think about things, isn't it?

If I could write these words to you, Susanne, write them in a letter so that somehow you could read and understand what you've done to me, then it would be easier to write. If I could grovel and beg and go on my knees to get a word with you – even a moment of seeing you! – I would do that. Susanne, I miss you.

Never, never have I loved like this – you are my companion even now, and you could have lived in the world as I know it, been my fellow-traveler.

No, I can't remember it all. I remember other things more easily. I remember the smell of the food, cloying, which led me to burn the cartons in the sink. I was covered in ash and the house smelled like damp, greasy smoke when Susanne knocked.

And before that.

I remembered things as I watched the fire. Dr Wall sitting there so knowingly, saying, 'Kolya, in all these sessions, you've tried to tell me that the other children don't like you because you're Russian. Don't you know that you're an American? You were born here.'

Ah, a moment of enlightenment. Yes, I belong here more than anywhere else in the world. This means that there is nowhere else to go, I am as comfortable as I will ever be. *That* relieved my mind.

I laughed at that one. Funny, funny. And I poured another vodka to enjoy it even more.

I can laugh at Dr Wall now. What a card, what a slapstick comedian with his pad and pencil and twitching cheek, and he never even knew it. He has no idea that I can laugh at him now.

And, ho-ho, he asked me, 'Do you ever hallucinate, Kolya?'

'No.'

'Never? Never have little dreams while you're awake that seem real?'

'You've asked me this question every few months for years. No, no, no.'

'We've been talking for years and yet you don't tell me anything. I am frustrated sometimes, I can't reach you. How can I reach you?'

'There's nothing to tell.'

'You've changed. You seem to be even more unhappy now. You were angry and confused when you first came to me and now you're bitter. Do you feel that? Do you want to be bitter?'

'You exaggerate everything, doctor. I'm not crazy, either. I'm just not like you, your nephews, or your next-door-neighbors.'

'Who do you want to be like?' he asked.

'I'll send you the pattern and cloth as soon as I find him.'

What a clever kid I was. When, later, I told Susanne about that one, I messed it up in the telling, but she laughed at the punchline just the same.

My life came to me in chunks of memory. I remembered being a small child, going to the department store with my mother, and losing hold of her hand. Instead of being frightened, I thought, I am free! And I passed the bins of toy trucks and five-cent dollies; I passed the tables of underwear and woolen scarves. I went outside onto Six-teenth Street, where the Christmas lights hung over the snowy streets. I toddled to Tremont and leaned over the rail, watching the ice skaters in Zekendorf Plaza. I wanted to skate more than anything in the world. When I asked the man if I could borrow some skates, he wanted money. So I just watched a woman in a short red skirt with white skates going round and round the rink, all her visible flesh pink with cold, her hair frizzy with ice shavings flying up in a mist around her twirls.

I would recognize her if I saw her today – but only if she looked the same as at that moment.

I remembered drinking beer with a girl in high school in the parking lot of a shopping center. Some of her crowd saw us together and drove over. We sat on bumpers and fenders drinking. Eventually, the guys started a whizzing contest, which I won. I felt such a part of the crowd to be able to out-pee them. Then, one of the boys said, 'Your witch doctor give you that to keep the demons off?'

Mikhail's jade that I wore around my neck had come out of my shirt. I took it off that night and never wore it again, and it was lost shortly after that. I never spoke to any of them again, including the girl. I never forgave them because I lost the only thing left to us that was Mikhail's. I will look all my life for it, but fear it's lost for ever.

And my first semester at college, sitting on the porch of the boarding house, breathing sweet autumn smells, feeling like someone with a purpose in life (I was going to be a history teacher then), my mind drenched in cheap wine. One of the other residents was playing his guitar, and I was learning the harmonica.

Free, free of my past, I thought.

And that was when I saw the man walk by with the candle, and no one else looked. He stopped and nodded to me, but no one else saw. He held out his candle to me, but none of the candlelight fell on my housemates' faces.

I knew he wanted me to go his way, but I was free to stay where I was.

Free.

What about the night Susanne came to me? I was so drunk that when I heard the knock, I was afraid, and got a kitchen knife. I went to the door with the knife in my hand. When I saw her standing there, smiling, bald and orange and glowing as if a hundred candles had been set around her, I dropped the knife.

Her head glistened with raindrops. She came in.

I took her close and kissed her; she kissed me. Then she stood back, apart, her hands in her jacket pockets, just smiling and looking at me. She was tiny, frail.

'I love you,' she said, 'and I've come to say goodbye.'

'Oh, God, I love you, too,' I whispered.

She just nodded. 'May I have a drink?'

I poured her a drink. She sat down in the rocking chair,

just as she had done that first day she came to my place, rocking slowly back and forth. I settled at her feet.

'What were you doing?' she asked. 'I thought you'd be asleep. It's been hours since Jack came home.'

'I was very much awake when Jack left,' I said.

'It's not going right, is it?'

But I didn't have to say anything. She seemed to understand everything so well. Everything about me, anyway.

I told her that I had been thinking about myself, that it was my main interest in life. There was little else for me to think about, actually. I talked and talked to her – I think I even told her such things as how big and strong my grandfather's hands were, how much I loved him.

Susanne had no interest in the past, the present, or the future. She had no interest in anything in particular, but she listened to me and drank with me, as one would enjoy a magazine while waiting for a train.

She was suffering.

We went into the bedroom and lay together, dressed, on my bed. I held her hand, but she didn't want me to hold her more than that because she hurt 'everywhere.' I rubbed her scalp lightly and kissed her cheekbones, and smiled at her.

She started to talk a little. She told me about what she had been like as a girl, how wasted her life had been. She told me that she hated the sight of her family. They lived on, and they lived badly in many ways, and wouldn't even look her in the eye.

'My mind has been full of "ifs" in these past months,' she said, stroking my hand, which was on her shoulder. 'What if I had done this or that differently? What have I done to cause myself to get sick and die? Is it just meant to be, or are there reasons?'

I listened. The alcohol began to wear off. I was in sympathy with her. I felt it all – the dying. She stopped talking after a time, and we just lay there, awake, staring out of the window as the sky lightened, as the dogs began to bark, and those same birds that had been chattering the evening before when Jack and I dragged in the chairs now rose again.

That life was so remote.

Nothing seemed as important as the relief that was coming. Susanne became restless, turning, pulling her legs up, relaxing them again.

'Kolya, would you bring me a glass of water and my jacket?'

I got out of bed. It was difficult to move. I felt debilitated, very old. I brought her what she wanted. I held her up as she opened the jar of pills and sprinkled them out on her hand then, one by one, put them into her mouth and swallowed. It took a long time.

I kissed her. I flung myself with her, and we were going at last. This isn't what drives men mad, this simple drifting, drifting to the bottom. It is the abandonment felt by the others who don't experience this that is maddening.

'Kolya,' she whispered, 'I'll be thinking of you,' she said.

'Yes.' I let go of her hand. 'I will think of you.'

'Take me home,' she said. 'The keys are in my jacket.'

I picked her up. Her car was pulled into the drive. She murmured a little as I slid her into the front seat, but didn't open her eyes. I got into the driver's seat with the keys in my hand, uncertain about working the vehicle. I figured it out and drove slowly with the milkmen and early traffic to the Berdos' house.

She opened her eyes. 'Kolya,' she said, but when I picked her up again to carry her inside, she was unconscious.

The front door was unlocked. The house was quiet. I put Susanne on the sofa and sat on the floor beside her, watching her breathe.

I fell asleep, leaning against the sofa, but I

16 June

I died.

I didn't stir; I was crumbling to dust already. No more speaking, no more seeing, no more mornings for me. I have heard the stories of the dying seeing their lives roll past them, but that is not what happened. (The spirit that lingered around what was called Nicholas Alexandrovich was aware of Paul coming down the stairs and seeing Susanne. If it hadn't been for the strange dark color in her lips and eyelids and the slack way her head tilted back on the upholstered pillow, she would have seemed only asleep. She appeared uncomfortable, as if she'd been on her back, and rolled onto her side without adjusting her arms and legs.) I was suddenly altogether what I used to be, came to be, and am. I was the toddler sitting in the wet dirt under the kitchen window, hearing my father and grandfather laugh; I was the child, bewildered on the first day of school by foreign words such as 'desk' and 'tablet'; (I saw Paul looking at me, but I wasn't really there any more. I was searching for my companion's soul – where was she? Why couldn't I perceive her? Paul's face was near. He touched Susanne's leg. He was gone suddenly and there was a sound upstairs.) I was the lad who woke screaming in pure terror in a room of twenty mad children; I was the young man, angry at being refused a driver's license because of a history of uncontrollable seizures; ('What's happened?' asked Jack. She touched Susanne's face, then pulled her wrist out from under her. 'She's dead,' she said flatly. 'I know,' said Paul.) I was the stranger, the friend, the son, the lover, the student all in one, twenty-seven years of moments coalesced into a timeless mass of being; I listened to everyone I had ever encountered, and no matter how I felt, you all touched me deeply; ('What happened?' Paul asked. 'I can't believe it, she's dead,' said Jack. 'I loved her!' Paul squeezed his face into Jack's shoulder, shuddering, whining.) I was the one who hated and loved each passing human in accordance with their own self-hatred and self-love; I was all things at

193

once that I had ever been, judged, sealed, and now assigned to silence for ever. I had a memory of what it was like to live – hearing the voices of others, feeling the world through my fingertips, smelling, tasting, and watching, watching, watching . . . I knew the smell of roses and dung, and the inner secrets of you. There were no angels to take me, only greyness. ('Mama?' Julie said.) The fabric of the membrane between life and death grew thicker and more impenetrable as my memories of life and my idea of my self scattered. I became tinier and there was nothing left of me but a spark smaller than an atom. ('Mother's dead,' Jack said.)

The silence began, the silence whose beginning was marked by the sensation of a scream. The voice was a memory – the voice of a woman that I had once loved, when I could love.

My father and Ben kept me out of the hospital. Jack wanted to put me in; she said I needed help, serious help, and right now. Ben told me later how they had to fight her.

I would have been diagnosed as a catatonic this time, Ben guessed, and never would have been allowed outside again.

'Are you starting to remember things?' he asked me today, but I can't recall anything from the moment Jack started screaming at me until the morning I was sitting in bed and saw Ben. There are vague, dream-like glimpses of in-between, but I prefer to let them go.

I came aware knowing that I wasn't in my own bed. And not in a hospital. Somewhere else, dressed, lying on a coverlet in someone's bedroom.

Looking right at Ben. What was he doing here, I wondered? His eyes were intensely dark and familiar. I raised my hand to cover my eyes because I couldn't face him.

'No, it's all right,' he said, pulling my hand down. 'You haven't done anything wrong. It's all right.'

I trusted him because it didn't matter any more.

17 June

Susanne left me behind. I wanted to go with her, but she left me.

I wonder at it. I hold her memory and play it over and over again. Sometimes I get confused and see Jack's face superimposed on Susanne's, but I know the difference. I'm not as confused as they think I am.

When I first started talking, Ben just nursed me. He would leave to teach his class and do a little work, but he hired someone to come and sit with me during those hours. I remember that stranger's face. I stared and stared at it, trying to make sense of it, but to no avail. It stared back at me, sometimes startling me when it moved or made a sound, but generally it was very quiet.

The truth is, I took comfort in having Ben around. I like him, like his care, and felt relief in the surrender. My father came sometimes, but he is made of dough, and the dough dries and hardens if it doesn't get back to the bakery every now and then for some new gluten, so he never stayed long.

My classes were dropped; Patricia sent me a get-well card, which I couldn't understand. What does a kitten and a ball of yarn have to do with Susanne, I wondered?

This is a copy of a tape recording that Ben made, which I have listened to several times:

'Just talk, forget it's there.' (Ben)

'Don't feel like talking.' (N.A.)

'Then we'll sit here and relax. Would you like some coffee?'

'*Da.*'

'No. No Russian. Let's speak English.'

'Look how reformed I am – hot coffee.'

'Kolya, have you ever wondered how I got interested in your family?'

'Ah, what a prize we are.'

'Yes, but all that stuff always just seemed like a crock of shit to me.'

'The tape recorder, doctor.'

'I'll edit it. Seriously, I would be the last person to believe all this. But I do think that ultra-sensitivity to others can make one psychotic. We aren't meant to be that close. And now, knowing you, and how you've been labeled and treated, I am really wondering how many people called paranoid schizophrenic may have started just by being psychic.'

'I never met anyone else that I thought was like me.'

'Well, who knows? You weren't exactly in shape to be investigating when you were institutionalized, were you?'

'No . . . ' Long pause. 'So?'

'What?'

'There's more to it, then. When you were telling the story about Mikhail, I sensed something personal about it.'

'Yes. I have a confession. I have been looking for your family for personal reasons.'

'What? You're not empathic, I know that.'

'No. My children are Mikhail Nicholaevich's great-grandchildren.'

'That's impossible.'

'No, it isn't. It's very possible, and true.'

'He never had family.'

'Well, not in the traditional sense, no, but he was a charming young man. Katherine's mother was conceived in the Dals' barn.'

'I don't believe it.'

'Doesn't matter what you believe. I don't know if you were aware of Mikhail's penchant for wanderers and travel-ing families. Not too long before your family's tragedy, Katherine's family was uprooted by a pogrom. They took shelter in the barn for more than a week. It was a bad spring storm. The family was so grateful to be protected that they were afraid to say anything when their 15-year-old daughter slipped away with Mikhail every night. Besides, she wasn't being forced, he was kind to her. I don't think Mikhail was ever brutal or forceful, but he did like to sleep with her. Maybe it was just this once – I don't know. How could we know that now? But that young girl is in her seventies now and still speaks of Mikhail as an angel that saved them.'

'Angel of death.'

'She says that he even begged her father to let her marry him. Seems that the Dals pick their women quickly.'

'Yes. And lose them quickly.'

'So, she had a baby girl, who grew up and had only Katherine, who is my wife, and we have a boy and a girl.'

'So, you are telling me . . . '

'My son is a direct descendant, and he is empathic.'

'He has *pozhar-golava?*'

A long silence, the sound of a match striking.

'What is he like?'

'He's different from the other kids, I suppose. He's mature. He's moody. He's in the yeshiva, wants to be a rabbi. With his special ability, he thinks he can help people.'

'Oh, pah, another Alexander Fyodorovich. The social worker from the dark side of the soul.'

'I think the contempt you have for your father is not deserved.'

'He's a failure.'

'So are you.'

'Yes, but I'm . . . was . . . trying to be something.'

'Yeah, well, you were getting a college education, but you are less able to take care of yourself than he is.'

'I've given that up, now, haven't I? I've given myself to science.'

'No. I won't take responsibility for your life. I am only going to try to find ways for you to manage what you call the dark side of your soul.'

'So, your son will go crazy trying to help people. Don't let him do that. It's all right if he's being sympathetic with bored little old ladies or men that are worried about their jobs, but what about the serious stuff? How is he going to sit in a roomful of people with a dying man? Has be been around death?'

'That's how we found out. Katherine's father died when Michael . . . '

'Michael.'

'Yes. When he was five or so. He passed out, had a seizure, fever – the whole routine that you know so well. We took him to a neurologist, a friend of mine and he found nothing. We took him to a psychiatrist, a friend of mine and he said there was nothing visibly wrong with him. Through testing and interviews, they found that he had a really startling sort of sensitivity to other people's feelings. We confused empathy and sympathy for a while and thought Michael was a sensitive boy. But they aren't the same, are they?'

'No.'

'When Katherine's grandmother found out, she became very upset. She said that Mikhail had told her about the Dals' ability, but she hadn't believed it. It never showed up in her daughter, and she'd forgotten about it. Then I started asking some of the Soviet Jews that had come from those parts. About five years ago, I met someone who knew part of the story, and have been able to piece together more since then. I never have told Katherine's grandmother what became of her mysterious Mikhail. And if you should meet her, please, don't tell her. It would break her heart. She's loved him for sixty years or more. Of course, she never married and was a disgraced woman. She had the child and kept it, and never gave up her ideal lover.'

'Katherine and Michael and . . . your daughter . . . they're our cousins.'

'That's right.'

'The rabbi-to-be, what does he think of having goyisher relatives?'

'He's anxious to meet you.'

'Oh.'

'What's the matter?'

'He'll like Papa, and maybe he'll like Grandmama.'

'But you don't think he'll like you?'

'I'm not very good with people under drinking age.'

'Listen to me, you can sit and have a bottle of wine between you when you meet, I promise. My son can drink, too. He's always craved liquor. I always thought him so righteous because he was hell to manage at all times except the holidays. During the holidays, passing the wine, saying the prayers, he became an angel.'

We laughed.

'You know, this all indicates that there is a physiological basis. If alcohol and drugs can shut it off, it has become sort of physical reality. Overloading you does damage – fevers, seizures. Perhaps it's located near your hypothalamus.'

'Yes, well, whatever. Have you studied your son – medically?'

'Some. I wanted to wait until he was older, more able to understand what he is consenting to, what we want from him. And I think we all wanted to wait until we found you. We've been looking for a long time, but it didn't take long once we found that your grandfather moved from New York to Denver. That was the tough fact to uncover.'

'Does he have grey eyes?'

'No. Brown. What's the matter, Kolya? What are you thinking?'

'Nothing.'

'I see.'

'I don't have to tell you everything I'm thinking, do I?'

'You know better than that.'

I was thinking of you, Susanne, and how much I miss seeing you. I think of how irretrievably gone you are, and I wonder what it was that you thought of – you promised that it would be of me – and what your dreams were as you found the end, that lovely, lovely end that you finally drifted down into. I had you, I was with you until then, and you passed on through without taking me. I should have taken pills with you. And I remember those pretty pills in your little, bony hand and the look in your eyes as you spilled them out and ate them one by one, knowing that this would get you there. I was thinking of you, Susanne, as I will be as long as I am still on this side.

I was remembering the raindrops sparkling on the silver fuzz on your scalp.

I was remembering sitting with you outside the Denver Public Library, looking at you in a blouse with embroidered flowers, admiring your lovely hair, and your dark, dark eyes. And the first time I touched you. And when we shared the wine. And when we talked in the lawn chairs, our faces so close . . .

I miss you, I miss you.

'There is something I have been meaning to tell you. About the story. It's a little different.'

'Oh? How's that?' Ben asked.

'You apparently have heard a variation of what my grandfather told the police. Of course, that's all you would be able to know. But, you may as well hear the truth of it. Mikhail came into my grandfather's rooms. First, he killed my aunt, Vera. Then he stabbed my father in the shoulder – my father complains about that shoulder still when the weather is bad. Fyodor stopped him then, trying to reason with him, trying to calm him down. Mikhail was determined to wipe the whole family out as a favor to mankind. Anyway, Fyodor had to kill him and throw him in the lake. He didn't commit suicide, or just "walk into the lake" – my grandfather killed him.'

'I see.'

'That's what I've been told. By my father.'

'Do you doubt it?'

'I don't know. Well, no, I don't doubt what I've told you.'

'What do you doubt?'

'I think that Grandfather may have killed others. He and Mikhail were very close, and I think Mikhail may have driven him to slaughter, too, but he had to stop when it came to his own children.'

'Why do you think that?'

'It's just a possibility.'

'Something you've sensed.'

'Yes. Something preying there in the background in all our lives. No one ever talked about it. No one. My father is very confused about the telling of his sister's murder. When

200

he told me about it, even when I was small, I sensed a lie somewhere.'

'It would be hard to lie to you, wouldn't it?'

'I don't know. I mean, if a person believes something as they tell me, or if I'm drunk . . . I'm not impervious to untruth.'

'This possibility bothers you a lot, doesn't it?'

'Yes.'

'Why?'

'Imagine if I were to be put in jail with a psychotic killer. I would begin to feel like him, which might lead to thinking and doing like him. I became all the psychoses and neuroses in the hospital and the school. I can't always distinguish between myself and the rest of the world.'

'I understand.'

'Papa likes being an empath. He has always been determined to use it to advantage, to read people, anticipate what would please them. He has a terror of angry people. In fact, I think . . . '

'What?'

'He moved out of our house . . . Well, I lost my temper with him once. I had a rotten temper, I guess. I was drunk, and he said something about a girl that lived down the street that I had been watching. I was sensitive about things like that in those days.'

Pause.

'Go on.'

'I used him, knowing that he was afraid of me. I found that I had power over him. I made Miranda go away with my anger. There was a long time of powerlessness when I was with the crazies, but when I got out, I had all sorts of anger and I bullied him. I still can. He's afraid of me.'

'That bothers you.'

'Yes, it frightens me when I'm angry. But I can't help it. He seems to ask for me to get upset, to incite me to do it. He cringes, he forgives, and he is the gentlest person in the world.'

'You became the one with the knife, didn't you?'
'I'm tired of talking now.'

19 June

Ben says to keep on writing. A rabbit in a trap, scribbling on the bottom of the cage. He talked me into showing him some of my journal, but had trouble deciphering the Dal dialect. This suddenly becomes like writing a term paper, I grope for the words to express things. I don't think I'll show him any more. I must not think of *them* as I write.

Ben was surprised when he read my reactions to him prowling around the house that night. Seems so long ago! He said if he'd had any idea I was so adept, he wouldn't have done it. What it was, he said, was trying to get up the nerve to knock. But he wanted to make sure I was alone. He walked around, sort of peering into windows, saw Jack, and went away.

He said that he thinks Papa and I are more 'developed' than his son. We had each other to play games with, to explore ranges and stretch our powers. He wonders if Michael will increase his ability with contact.

Contamination, I said.

Ben, in his wearily patient way, sighed and said something about sharing. I hate some of the words that these people use. They have changed a little since I was in therapy before, but they have the same well-balanced feel to them. And not much power. Sharing. Sharing *this*? Whatever for?

I haven't talked to him about Susanne yet. I've never told anyone what I felt or knew of you, Susanne. It is too deep to come out easily.

Am going home with Ben after the semester is over. He has two friends, Dr Watts and Dr Blau, who are both going to work on me. I asked him what they will do, and he said neurological tests, scans, nerve conduction. But I sign a consent for each test. Anything that looks fishy to me, I can refuse. I am not committed, I am not arrested, I am not legally anything to these people except interesting. I can walk away any time, he says.

That's a relief.

I don't know how I said yes, or if I ever did. It doesn't matter any more. Maybe I do need help.

Help!

But it's strange. I do feel better already, although I am afraid of feeling better, too.

I asked him – since he believes that it's physiological – if he could cut it out of me. He laughed a little, thinking I was joking. But it seems as logical as my vasectomy (which now, of course, seems a futile gesture – Mikhail may have grandchildren all over the world, so I haven't ended it after all).

'You'd miss it, but I don't think that's possible anyway.'

Papa came last night and talked to Ben for hours. They talked a lot about Mikhail, about the whole thing. His story hasn't changed, and I watched him carefully and still felt a little lie. But he was so young, how would he know? Papa cried, which made me cry, too. I got up and went out on the balcony of the apartment and watched a couple swimming and a woman sunning herself, even though the daylight was nearly gone. I thought about Susanne, but it is hurting less. I can breathe just a little bit again, but I still have this *loneliness*.

Papa asked me not to be angry with him because he didn't protect me better. What does it matter now?

I found out that Jack was asking about me every day that she worked with Ben. But she has never tried to visit me.

Ben said I should learn to swim. I wore a pair of cut-off jeans and stood in the pool up to my waist this afternoon. It was hell.

21 June

I am back in my house for these last weeks before I go away with Ben. Katherine has finally arrived. My cousin Katherine. She is all right, but we don't feel a lot of kinship right at the moment, I don't think.

It feels good to be alone again. I am stretching and staying up late, getting back to my habits, my old life again.

Last night, I called Jack. It was late; apparently, I woke her father, but she agreed to come and see me. I stood outside my house, waiting for her. She pulled up in front of the house and got out. She leaned on the side of the truck and looked at me.

I was feeling shy of her. 'Let's take a walk,' I said, not wanting to go inside.

We started up the sidewalk. All those weeks that had come between us seemed to have undone the months together and we were as new to each other as we had been in the spring.

'How are you?' she asked.

'I'm all right. I really am. Feeling pretty good.'

'Good,' she said. 'You look okay.'

She was keeping pace with me, but I realized that I was walking too fast for her to be conversational. I slowed down. I didn't really know what I wanted to talk to her about.

'How's your family?' I asked.

'Fine. Dad's going back to work on Monday. He'll be better when he's busy.'

'Yeah.'

'Kolya, I wish I knew what to say to you. Everything just seemed to happen at the wrong times, and I still don't understand *what* happened. I wish things had worked out better because I really care a lot about you.'

'You *loved* me,' I said.

'I did. But, well, I loved part of you. The rest – I don't know. It's as if there are about five of you, and I only know one and the other four kept doing things I didn't like.'

I was feeling the nightmare of a child in one of the houses we passed and it gave me a shudder. 'Let's go back.'

I felt oppressed once we reached the house. Actually, I didn't know what to do with her.

I told her the truth this time. I asked her if she remembered the story about the family that Ben had told that night. Yes, she remembered. 'That was my family. That is why I had trouble in the hospital and knew that I had to get out.'

Jack sat silently. She asked no questions, she made no comments.

'What do you say?' I finally asked.

'What *can* I say?' She shook her head. 'I've misinterpreted everything all the way down the line. I've never understood anything, I've been misled and not trusted.'

'No, Jack, it isn't quite like that.'

She began to cry then.

I sat for a few moments, watching her. I was beginning to feel agitated. First of all, when I looked at her eyes, the shape of her face, I was seeing someone else. It hurt again, to see your daughter's eyes looking so much like yours. And then, I knew how much I'd hurt her, and now the reasoning seemed so false.

I stood and stepped toward her.

'Why didn't you tell me?' she screamed at me.

I stopped. 'I was afraid you'd tell Ben.'

I reached for her.

'DON'T TOUCH ME!' She flinched under my fingers.

Terrors – I'm not sure whose, perhaps both of ours.

'And what about my mother?'

I sat. 'Your mother?'

'Why were you there?'

I smiled because somehow it made it a link between us, even Jack knew that there was a connection. 'I'll tell you, Susanna Pavlovna, I just hope that when I finally die I don't have to find strangers to go to for the last bit of love and affection that is left in me.'

'Bastard,' she said.

'I already regret saying that. I'm sorry.'

We stood apart. Jack was pale except for a pink mask around her eyes. I pitied her because she didn't want the truth after all, not like this.

'Why don't you gather up the things that are yours and go. We don't need to be ugly, do we?'

She hung her head.

'Wait.' I thought of something, and in a desperate moment, I hurried to the bedroom. I opened the drawer and searched under the panties, the T-shirts, and found that piece of paper.

The photo.

A photo of a stranger. Not the Susanne that I had known at all. I put it back, disappointed. I had nothing except what was left inside me.

Jack followed. 'She told us that only one person in the world understood her and knew what she was going through. Only one. And I thought it might be me.' She laughed bitterly.

I hadn't been prepared for this. I could remember all the love that Jack had carried around with her, and now it was gone. What was the look in her eyes? Was her voice going to soften?

Sobbing, she began pulling things out of the drawers.

I went outside and had a cigarette.

It took her a long time. I sat down on the concrete porch and looked at what stars I could see shining through the city lights. And the dark shapes of the mountains. I could smell pine, and that incongruous beach smell that sometimes came in with the western winds.

She came out carrying a grocery bag, and went to her truck. I followed.

'Kolya, I'm sorry I made a scene.'

'It's all right. I understand.'

She came up close and regarded me. 'You knew how I felt all the time.'

'Yes.'

She nodded. 'It's all pretty embarrassing in retrospect.

Like finding out that you've been seen naked every day without knowing it, even though you believe in the beauty of the human body. I've tried to be honest, but I didn't even have to be.' She shook her head in thought. 'Why?'

'Why what?'

'Why did you love me?'

I pulled a strand of her hair through my fingers. How like your eyes are hers sometimes, when she isn't being restless, searching, decisive. 'Because you forgave Richard the Third,' I said.

She laughed. 'And I loved you because . . . I don't know. You are different, interesting.' She shrugged. 'My mother liked you. Maybe that's why, too.'

'She loved you, Jack,' I said.

Jack scuffed at the sidewalk with her toe.

'Would you mind,' I asked softly, 'if I send you a postcard every now and then? And maybe we could get together for coffee when I come back?'

'Sure,' she said, looking up with wet eyes. But there wasn't much conviction in either of us for a future.

We kissed and she left.

How many times have I watched those truck tail lights move away from me, and this is all gone, changed now.

This morning, I told Ben all about Susanne.

June 23

Dear Nicholas,

My father has written to me about you. He says that you have troubles like mine. I'm looking forward to meeting you. You've had your father to explain a lot. I'm not saying that my father hasn't been understanding, but I'm sure you can imagine how lonely it is, and how happy I am to find you, my cousin.

If you come to visit us, you can stay in my room. I don't mind sleeping on the sofa. Do you think we could write to each other? I love history, too. Maybe we have a lot in common.

Sincerely,

Michael Miller

PS Tonight, Dad called and told me that you are sad because you lost your friend, Susanne. I didn't know before. I'll light my candle for her.